KB201793

금관의 예수

희곡 금관의 예수

초판 1쇄 발행 2022년 5월 10일

지 은 이 | 이동진
영　　역 | 이동진
펴 낸 곳 | 해누리
펴 낸 이 | 김진용
편집주간 | 조종순
디 자 인 | 종달새
마 케 팅 | 김진용

등 록 | 1998년 9월 9일 (제16-1732호)
등록변경 | 2013년 12월 9일 (제2002-000398호)
주 소 | 서울시 영등포구 당산로 20길 13-1
전 화 | (02) 335-0414 팩스 | (02) 335-0416
전자우편 | haenuri0414@naver.com

ISBN 978-89-6226-127-1(03810)

1972년 국내 초연 50주년 기념 단행본

금관의 예수

지음 · 영역 이동진

Jesus of Gold Crown

해누리

차례

「금관의 예수」 참고사항

1

이 희곡은 극단 '상설무대'(대표 이동진)가 1972년 1월 21일부터 2월 10일까지 서강대학교 운동장의 야간 야외공연을 비롯하여 원주 · 수원 · 대전 · 광주 · 대구 · 부산 등지의 가톨릭회관에서 순회공연, 3월 초 드라마센터(서울)에서 2회 공연함으로써 당시 교회와 사회에 적지 않은 파문을 일으킨 작품이다.

2

드라마센터 공연을 관람한 희곡작가 유치진 선생과 평론가 유민영 교수가 1972년 3월 12일자 가톨릭교회의 유일한 주간신문인 『가톨릭시보』에 연극평을 크게 게재한 바 있다.(12쪽 이하 참고)

3

1972년 2월 26일자로 문공부 산하 한국예술문화윤리위원회에 접수번호 제24호로 접수된 이 희곡의 원 제목이 「청동 예수」였으나 극단 상설무대 회원들의 의견에 따라 공연될 때의 제목을 「금관의 예수」로 변경하였다.

4

여기 정리한 희곡은 1972년 당시 공연된 내용을 있는 그대로 충실히 담은 것이며 위원회에서 삭제했던 대목도 다시 수록하였다. 나오는 사람들의 배역도 1972년 당시 출연했던 연기자들의 성명임을 아울러 밝혀둔다.

5

이 희곡을 새삼스럽게 정리하는 이유는 이 희곡의 공연이 1972년 당시 가톨릭교회와 지성인들의 각성을 촉구했다는 역사적 의미를 재음미하고 싶다는데 있을 뿐 아니라 극도로 어려운 여건 아래에서도 소극

장 운동에 헌신했던 상실무대 회원 모두에게 희곡작가로서 따뜻한 정을 보내고 싶기 때문이다. 상설무대에서 뛰던 회원들이 다시 모여 극단 '연우무대'를 만든 것은 결코 우연한 결과가 아닐 것이다.

6

1972년 당시 공연에서 연출은 최종율, 조연출은 백승규가 맡았다. 그리고 대한가톨릭학생총연합회(지도신부 박상래)가 재정적으로 지원하였다.

1989년, 이동진

추기:

이 희곡은 한국희곡작가협회의 「1989년도 연간 희곡집」과 이동진 희곡 모음 「누더기 예수」(동산출판사, 1991)에 수록되었고, 영역본 원고는 나이지리아의 「Spectrum Books Limited」 출판사가 1999년에 라고스(Lagos)에서 단행본으로 출판하였다.

Author's Notes in the English text

I wrote this play on the night of December 31st, 1971, at my small roon in Changchon-dong, Seoul, Korea. After finishing the manuscript, I remember, I added my frank thoughts as follows:

"The most serious of problems that the Korean Catholic Church now faces is the fact that Christians do not live according to their faith nor practise the love and justice of Jesus. It is a regrettable reality that they are idle even in their self-examination of the cause. From this viewpoint, I tried to pursue the true essence of Jesus.

"I can't fathom how much and concretely my efforts were expressed in this play. It is true, however, I did not spare my best to express as honestly as possible.

"I ardently desire that all those who serve Our Lord only with their lips should disappear, and that Christ's teaching become not a decoration article, but truly the basis of living faith. I remember the words of an Apostle: The faith without an action is dead faith."

In February, 1989, eighteen years after the play's first performance, I rearranged it for the record in the Hague. At that time I was a Counsellor of the Korean Embassy there. And when it was included in my fourth collection of plays, "Jesus in the Rags", which was published in August 1991 in Seoul, I added a note written in the Hague as follows:

"During the last two decades, our society, and the Korean Catholic Church, too, has comparatively profited by the fruit of economic development, but, discovering the reality of nowadays that still embraces not a few corners of darkness I cannot help myself but feel some bitterness and sorrow. The past eighteen years tried to teach us that the mental poverty and the barrenness of soul were more terrible things than the poverty in material terms or the physical oppression. It is to be examined how much lessons we have learnt from the past.

"Anyway, the more this play is welcome by the audience, or the more deeply it moves them, then, the more hopelessly our society reveals its illness. Chewing this fact, I, as the author, feel great sadness and some pride as well. I wish our society to turn, as quickly as possible, into a more just one where this play would be rather neglected by the audience."

The play was performed for the first time by a theatre group, "The Permanent Stage" (Representative: Lee Dong-Jin), from February 6th to March 3rd, 1972, in Korean cities including Seoul. The first performance was directed by Choi Jong-Yul with the assistance of Paik Seung-Gyu.

Very controversial, famous or notorious (to the military), it has been performed many times in Korea, but was not published during the long period of military rule. The contents of the play have been discussed and quoted in not a few articles of the Liberation theology and the Minjoong(People) theology in Korea and beyond.

After the rearrangement of 1989, it was included in the "Annual Collection of Plays(1989)" by the Korean Playwrights Association.

In Korea and beyond, the authorship of this play has been wrongly ascribed to the well known poet, Kim Ji-Ha. This was in spite of the Catholic Weekly report of March 12, 1972. This error of authorship was probably due to my long stay abroad or the fact that the play's publication in a book form took so long to come.

Recently my real authorship was reported again by leading Korean newspapers and a monthly such as the Catholic Newspaper (Sep. 1st, 1991), Donga Daily Newspaper (Aug. 8th, 1991), Kookmin Daily Newspaper (Aug. 17th, 1991) and the Monthly Queen (April, 1993).

풍자극 金冠의 예수

이동진 作. 최종률 演出

偽善的그리스도人을 질책

1개월간 全國을 巡回공연

【서울】사회정의구현과아울러 교회쇄신을위해 전개됐던한국「빠스토마나」주최「크리스찬문화운동」은 2월6일 원주를 비롯, 8일 수원아카데미, 11일광주가톨릭문화관, 13일 부산 데레사여고, 16일 대전가톨릭문화관서각각개최됐는데 특히 이번 처음으로 시도된 문화운동 프로그램중 연극 이동진작 최종률연출「金冠의 예수」는 공연한곳마다 관객들의 절찬을받았다.

더욱 원주서는 당일2회의연속공연이있었고 대전서는 대전 MBC방송국「총정의 메아리」시간에 중계되어 일반시민들에게까지 깊은감명을주었다.

거의 1개월간의 지방순회를 마친후 서울에서는지난3일드라마센터에서 오후3시와 7시, 2회에 걸쳐 공연됐는데 성직자 평신도는물론 가톨릭의정의구현운동에 관심을모으고있는자및 저명인사들이 참석, 연극계의 보기드문 성황을 이루었다.

또한 관중들은 장이바뀔때 마다 구구절절 신랄한풍자적 연기에 박수갈채를보냈으며 단하루 만의 공연을아쉬워했다.

그런데「금관의예수」는 허식과위선에 가득찬껍데기 그리스도인에대한 날카로운 질책을 목표로한 작품이다.

우리들世上에神은 오직하나… 진실한 사랑·정의·아픔·눈물이 하나이듯이神의 얼굴은 늘 같다. 그러나 그의代理人들…

簡潔해도 깊은 秀作

格下돼가는 敎會 신랄히 비판

演劇評 柳致眞

한국「빠스토마나」주최인 연극「金冠의예수」공연을3월3일밤 드라마센터극장에서 보았다. 舞台에는 머리에金冠을얹은 콩크리트製實物大의 예수立像하나 그立像주변에서는 문둥이·거지·창녀·순경·사장·수녀·신부등 가지각색의 人間相이 우글거려 오늘의사회의 病弊를 풍자한다.

그러나 예수는 외롭다.

왜?

예수는黃金이나 權力에눈이어두운者들에게 둘러싸여 그들이自己의 욕심을채우기위하여 예수를팔며, 그러기위하여 立像의머리위에 金冠을 씌워놓고있는 것이다. 정작 예수의사랑과 자비가必要한 사람들—굶주리고 헐벗고 가난한사람들에게서는 멀리 격리되어 그들에게 아무런영향을 주지못하고있기 때문이다.

病者와 굶주림에 못견디던 문둥이가 하루는 콩크리트예수의立像 머리위에서 金冠을 발견한다. 그黃金덩어리가 탐이나서 훔치려든다. 콩크리트立像은 입을연다. 『가시冠이 마땅한 내게는 金冠은無用하다. 그金冠을가지고가라. 이왕이면내 全身을 싸고있는 콩크리트마저 벗겨 나를黃金狂과權力狂으로부터 해방시켜 나를 病들고 가난하고 외로운사람들의 친구가되게 해달라」는것이다.

이얼마나 오늘의格下되어가는 敎會에대한 대담하고 신랄한 비판인가? 간결한가운데 깊고 함축성있는 秀作이다. 이作者(이동진)의 장래가 촉망된다.

이공연에 즈음하여 發表한「가톨릭문화운동」이란취지문에서 한국「빠스토마나」는 이렇게외쳤다.

『하느님앞에서평등한인간, 죄악에서 해방되어 완전히 자유스러워진인간, 편견없이 서로사랑하는 인간, 어떠한 댓가로도 매매될수없는 인간, 궁극에 가서는 하느님과 일치되어야하는 인간

가톨릭의 이상이 추구하는 인간像을 구현하기위한 적극적인 활동만이 가톨릭문화창조의 원천이될 것이고 조직적이고 집중적인문화운동」을통해서만 형성될수 있다.

현실에 존재하는 교회는 영원히불완전한 교회이다. 이땅의가톨릭적 상황은 정말 가난하고 병들고 버림받은 소외당한 사람들에게 우선적으로 봉사하고 있는가?」

「金冠의예수」는以上의「빠스 토마나」의 정신을적절하게 무대화했다. 가톨릭문화운동의 건전한앞날에 기대하며 이연극집단의 장래성에 크게기대한다.

〈극작가〉

宗敎의 無力 꾸짖어

現實的가톨릭의苦惱를 보는듯

演劇評 柳敏榮

3월3일「드라마센터」에서는 색다른크리스찬文化행사가있었다. 한국「빠스토마나」주최, 가톨릭시보사와한국정의평화위원회후원으로「金冠의예수」(이동진작최종률연출)라는 가톨릭批判劇을 공연한 것이다. 예수서고상과 문둥이·걸인부부그리고 神父와修女를 등장시켜 황금만능주의에의한 社會正義의 타락과 위선, 또 이와같이 부패한社會現實앞에서의 宗敎의갈등과 無力을매도한 작품을 바로가톨릭단체에서 주최하여 공연한것은 확실히충격적이다.

演劇은 행동의예술이기때문에 대중에게 직접적이고 또빠르게 영향을준다. 그래서 宗敎단체에서는 옛날부터 전교의수단으로 연극을 많이이용해왔다. 그러니까종교단체에서하는연극내용이란 대개가 종교의 숭고성과존엄성 나아가서는 神性으로써 敎訓的인것이었다. 그리고 非宗敎人이쓰고 일반극단에서 종교를테마로한작품을공연할때는 거의종교의위선 無氣力과 타락을질타하는것이 상례였다. 그러나대표적인 경우가제2차세계대전중「나찌스」가유대인을학살할때 교황청이 방관했다고하여 가톨릭(神)의침묵을 비판한「神의代理人」(롤후호크후트作)이 바로그것이다. 어느개인이건단체이건간에 그들자신의 恥部를 외부에 드러내지 않으려는것이 본능이다. 그런데도가톨릭단체에서 그들손으로現實의不正과 不條理앞에가톨릭의 無氣力을 고발한내용의연극을 무대에올린것은확실히 충격적이고 용감한것이었다.

작금의 가톨릭 社會正義운동과 관련하여 생각할때 오늘날과 같은 韓國現實속에서의 가톨릭의 고뇌를보는듯하여 가슴이 뭉클했다. 宗敎의 究極의목표중의하나가 社會正義의實現이라고볼때 종교가항상 스스로를 매질하는것은 퍽바람직한 일이다. 우리나라 가톨릭이 서양에서 伝來하여 土着할때 상당히많은피를흘린伝統을갖고있기때문에「金冠의예수」가 신랄히비판한것처럼 한국가톨릭敎會가다른종교처럼 그렇게 부패했다고는 보지않는다. 作品자체는 퍽未熟하다. 대개풍자극에서는 상징적인手法을쓰는데「金冠의예수」는 풍자극이면서도 리얼리즘적인正攻法을쓰고있어 演劇으로서는 생경하고 세련되지못한 감을주었다.

〈연극평론가〉

『가톨릭시보』(1972. 3. 12. 자)

■ 『가톨릭시보』 1972년 3월 12일 기사 내용 전문

풍자극 「금관의 예수」

이동진 작 · 최종률 연출

위선적 그리스도인을 질책
1개월간 전국을 순회공연

【서울】 사회정의구현과 아울러 교회쇄신을 위해 전개됐던 한국 〈빡스 로마나〉 주최 〈크리스찬문화운동〉은 2월 6일 원주를 비롯, 8일 수원아카데미, 11일 광주 가톨릭문화회관, 13일 부산 데레사여고, 16일 대전 가톨릭문화관서 각각 개최됐는데 처음으로 시도된 문화운동 프로그램 중 연극 이동진 작 최종률 연출 「금관의 예수」는 공연한 곳마다 관객들의 절찬을 받았다.

더욱 원주서는 당일 2회의 연속 공연이었고 대전서는 MBC방송국 〈충정의 메아리〉 시간에 중계되어 일반 시민에게까지 깊은 감명을 주었다.

거의 1개월간의 지방 순회를 마친 후 서울에서는 지난 3일 드라마센터에서 오후 3시와 7시, 2회에 걸쳐 공연됐는데 성직자, 평신도는 물론 가톨릭의 정의구현운동에 관심을 모으고 있는 자 및 저명인사들이 참석, 연극계의 보기 드문 성황을 이루었다.

또한 관중들은 장이 바뀔 때마다 구구절절 신랄한 풍자적 연기에 박수갈채를 보냈으며 단 하루만의 공연을 아쉬워했다.

그런데 「금관의 예수」는 형식과 위선에 가득 찬 껍데기 그리스도인에 대한 날카로운 질책을 목표로 한 작품이다.

■ 연극평_유치진

간결해도 깊은 수작

격하돼가는 교회 신랄히 비판

한국 〈빡스 로마나〉 주최인 연극 「금관의 예수」 공연을 3월 3일 밤 드라마센터극장에서 보았다. 무대에는 머리에 금관을 얹은 콩크리트 실물 크기의 예수 입상 하나, 그 입상 주변에서는 문둥이, 거지, 창녀, 순경, 사장, 수녀, 신부 등 가지각색의 인간상이 우글거려 오늘의 사회의 병폐를 풍자한다.

그러나 예수는 외롭다. 왜? 예수는 황금이나 권력에 눈이 어두운 자들에게 둘러싸여 그들이 자기의 욕심을 채우기 위하여 예수를 팔며, 그러기 위하여 입상의 머리 위에 금관을 씌워놓고 있는 것이다. 정작 예수의 사랑과 자비가 필요한 사람들 – 굶주리고 헐벗고 가난한 사람들에게서는 멀리 격리되어 그들에게 아무런 영향을 주지 못하고 있기 때문이다.

병고와 굶주림에 못 견디던 문둥이가 하루는 콩크리트 예수의 입상 머리 위에서 금관을 발견한다. 그 황금 덩어리가 탐이 나서 훔치려 든다. 콩크리트 입상은 입을 연다. "가시관이 마땅한 내 금관은 무용하다. 그 금관을 가지고 가라. 이왕이면 내 전신을 싸고 있는 콩크리트 마저 벗겨 나를 황금광과 권력광으로부터 해방시켜 나를 병들고 가난하고 외로운 사람들의 친구가 되게 해달라."는 것이다.

이 얼마나 오늘의 격하되어 가는 교회에 대한 대담하고 신랄한 비판인가? 간결한 가운데 깊고 함축성 있는 작이다. 이 작자(이동진)의 장래가 촉망된다.

이 공연에 즈음하여 발표한 '가톨릭문화운동'이란 취지문에서 한국 〈빡스 로마나〉는 이렇게 외쳤다.

"하느님 앞에서 평등한 인간, 죄악에서 해방되어 완전히 자유스러워진 인간, 편견 없이 서로 사랑하는 인간. 어떠한 댓가로도 매매될 수 없는 인간, 궁국에 가서는 하느님과 일치되어야 하는 인간. 가톨릭의 이상이 추구하는 인간을 구현하기 위한 적극적인 활동만이 가톨릭 문화창조의 원천이 될 것이고 조직적이고 집중적인 문화 '운동'을 통해서만 형성될 수 있다.

현실에 존재하는 교회는 영원히 불완전한 교회이다. 이 땅의 가톨릭적 상황은 정말 가난하고 병들고 버림받은 소외당한 사람들에게 우선적으로 봉사하고 있는가?"

「금관의 예수」는 이상의 〈빡스 로마나〉의 정신을 적절하게 무대화했다. 가톨릭 문화운동의 건전한 앞날에 기대하며 이 연극집단의 장래성에 크게 기대한다.

(극작가 유치진)

■ 연극평_유민영

종교의 무력 꾸짖어

현실적 가톨릭의 고뇌를 보는 듯

3월 3일 드라마센터에서는 색다른 크리스찬 문화행사가 있었다. 한국 〈빡스 로마나〉 주최, 가톨릭시보사와 한국정의평화위원회 후원으로 「금관의 예수」(이동진 작, 최종률 연출)라는 가톨릭 비판극을 공연한 것이다. 예수 석고상과 문둥이, 걸인 부부 그리고 신부와 수녀를 등장시켜 황금만능주의에 의한 사회정의의 타락과 위선, 또 이와같이 부패한 사회현실 앞에서의 종교의 갈등과 무력을 매도한 작품을 바로 가톨릭 단체에서 주최하여 공연한 것은 확실히 충격적이었다.

연극은 행동의 예술이기 때문에 대중에게 직접적이고 또 빠르게 영향을 준다. 그래서 종교단체에서는 옛날부터 전교의 수단으로 연극을 많이 이용해왔다. 그러니까 종교단체에서 하는 연극 내용이란 대개가 종교의 숭고성과 존엄성 나아가서는 신성으로써 교훈적인 것이었다. 그리고 비종교인이 쓰고 일반극단에서 종교를 테마로 한 작품을 공연할 때는 거의 종교의 위선 무기력과 타락을 질타하는 것이 상례였다. 그러나 대표적인 경우가 제2차세계대전 중 나찌스가 유대인을 학살할 때 교황청이 방관했다고 하여 가톨릭(신)의 침묵을 비판한 「신의 대리인」(톨후호크후트 작)이 바로 그것이다. 어느 개인이건 단체이건 간에 그들 자신의 치부를 외부에 드러내지 않으려는 것이 본능이다. 그런데 가톨릭단체에서 그들 손으로 현실의 부정과 부조리 앞에 가톨릭의 무기력을 고발한 내용의 연극을 무대에 올린 것은 확실히 충격적이고 용감한 것이었다.

자간의 가톨릭 사회정의운동과 관련하여 생각할 때 오늘날과 같은 한국 현실 속에서의 가톨릭의 고뇌를 보는듯하여 가슴이 뭉클했다. 종교의 궁극의 목표 중의 하나가 사회정의의 실현이라고 볼 때 종교가 항상 스스로를 매질하는 것은 퍽 바람직한 일이다. 우리나라 가톨릭이 서양에서 전래하여 토착할 때 상당히 많은 피를 흘린 전통을 갖고 있기 때문에 「금관의 예수」가 신랄히 비판한 것처럼 한국가톨릭교회가

다른 종교처럼 그렇게 부패했다고는 보지 않는다. 작품 자체는 퍽 미숙하다. 대개 풍자극에서는 상징적인 수법을 쓰는데 「금관의 예수」는 풍자극이면서도 리얼리즘적인 정공법을 쓰고 있어 연극으로서는 생경하고 세련되지 못한 감을 주었다.

(연극평론가 유민영)

우리들 세상에 신은 오직 하나…
진실한 사랑, 정의, 아픔, 눈물이 하나이듯이
신의 얼굴은 늘 같다.

| A PLAY |

JESUS OF GOLD CROWN

|희곡|

금관의 예수

The world premiere of「Jesus of Gold Crown」 was performed on the open ground of the Seogang University, Seoul, on the night of January 21, 1972 by the theatre group「Permanent Stage」. The cast was as follows:

Jesus of Gold Crown *Yoo Woo-Keun*
Priest *Song Ji-Hearn*
Sister *Lee Sook-Hee*
Leper *Yoon Sung-Hark*
Beggar *Lee Sang-Woo*
Prostitute *Kim Sun-Mi*
Old Woman *Hong Choog-Ok*
Policeman *Hwang In-Ki*
Woman in Black Clothes *replaced by the narration of the priest*

「금관의 예수」는 1972년 1월 21일 야간에
서울 소재 서강대학교의 운동장에서
극단「상설무대」에 의해 국내 최초로 공연되었다.
당시 배역은 아래와 같다.

금관의 예수 유우근
신부 송지헌
수녀 이숙희
문둥이 윤성학
거지 이상우
창녀 홍충옥
아주머니 김선미
경찰 황인기
검은 옷의 여인 신부의 해설로 가름했음

CHARACTERS

JESUS OF GOLD CROWN

PRIEST

SISTER

LEPER

BEGGAR

PROSTITUTE

OLD WOMAN

POLICEMAN

WOMAN IN BLACK CLOTHES

Time.

Middle of winter, supposedly, of January or February, 1972.

Place.

Act One *living room of a Catholic priest, Seoul*

Act Two *front street at the entrance of a Catholic church*

Act Three *front ground of the church.*

나오는 사람들

금관의 예수

신부

수녀

문둥이

거지

창녀

아주머니

경찰

검은 옷의 여인

때

어느 겨울(1972년 1월~2월을 상정)

곳

제1장 서울시내 어느 본당신부의 응접실

제2장 성당 입구 앞길

제3장 성당 마당

PROLOGUE

The title song *(originally written and composed by Kim Min-Ki)* starts to flow.

As the curtain rises, all characters appear on the stage moving around freely. A policeman in uniform chases after a beggar and a leper, both of whom run away desperately.

All lights out. The sound of wooden sticks hitting each other is heard as if a prophet's groan. Someone is beating a drum almost inaudibly, but more and more loudly, then, suddenly stops.

Dimmers in. Only a woman in black clothes remains on the stage who lifts, from time to time, her arms high in the air and narrates the following prologue like an incantation. She may freely sweep over the stage.

서설

김민기 작사 작곡의 '금관의 예수' 노래가 흘러나온다.

막이 오르면, 나오는 사람들이 모두 무대 위에 등장하여 각자 자유로운 동작을 보여준다. 경찰이 거지와 문둥이를 쫓아내려고 하면 거지와 문둥이는 필사적으로 달아나려고 한다.

조명이 나가면, 나무막대기의 둔탁한 소리가 마치 예언자의 신음처럼 들려온다. 북소리도 섞여 있다.

조명이 서서히 밝아지면, 검은 옷차림의 여인만 남아 하늘을 향해 때때로 두 팔을 높이 들어 올리면서 주문인 양 아래 서설을 읊어댄다. 여인은 자유롭게 무대를 휩쓸어도 좋다.

Woman in black clothes Do you know how the most sacred things are now? Ha! They are smeared by syphilis bacteria. This is an age when the greatest among all the names on earth is ridiculed. Everyday, under that very sun, crooked men are creating a tragedy always newer than the past. But no one dares show his courage to accuse them. What kind of an age this is! The age of ourselves!

Ah! Treacherous smiles of a hypocrite shake the centre of the good earth, and evil plots of a coward brandish bare daggers behind the back of those who love the truth. Then, what's happening? An angel, too ashamed, covers his eyes, while a devil dances at the head of a masked procession. The human reason turns into a slide of a kindergarten. In this age we can see nothing but orphanages without a signboard. What kind of an age this is! *(Pause. Starts a grotesque dance.)*

Where can we ever find out a home, today, like that of Nazareth? *(sighes)* The good earth, once fertile, is now so polluted by human

여인 가장 성스러운 것이 매독균으로 더럽혀지고 있습니다. 땅 위에서 가장 위대한 이름이 조롱을 당하고 있는 시대입니다. 사악한 사람들이 태양 아래 날마다 새로운 비극을 만들어 내는데도, 아무도 그것을 비난하는 용기 내보이지 못하는 시대! 우리들의 시대입니다.

아아, 위선자의 음흉한 미소가 대지의 심장에 이르고, 비겁한 자의 흉계가 진실을 사랑하는 사람의 등 뒤에서 칼날을 번뜩이니, 천사는 부끄러움으로 눈을 가리고, 악마가 가장행렬 선두에서 춤을 추고 있습니다. 인간 이성은 유치원 미끄럼틀이 되고, 눈에 보이는 것은 간판 없는 고아원뿐인 이 시대! (사이. 여인이 기괴한 춤을 춘다)

오늘 우리는 어디서 나사렛의 가정을 찾아볼 수 있겠습니까? (한숨) 비옥하던 대지가 이제는 인간의 피로 오염되었고, 다시는 곡식을 자라게 하지 않을 것입니다. 가장 강한 자가 책임을 깡그리 회피한 이상, 아무도 그 사

blood that it will never again make rice and wheat grow. Since the strongest man has already completely evaded completely his responsibility, no one will trust him anymore. Since the man who should be the truest goes about selling poison of flattery, no one will dare to tell the truth as it is.

Therefore, a son will distrust his father, a wife will have nothing to say against her husband's debauchery, a brother will not come forward to curse the flesh traffic and, at last, this land will turn into the hell of slaves and cowards.

(laughs hysterically)

However... The day will come. Surely the day will come when the heaven will open, wide open. On the day of Him who transcends all human beings, where will you, all of you, stand? On His left side? Otherwise, on the right? Will you belong to the blessed lines? Or, mixed with numerous devils who are cursed to everlasting existence, will you lower your head?

(thrusts her finger to the audience)

No room, not an inch for your chance of

람을 신뢰하지 않을 것입니다. 가장 진실해야 할 사람이 아첨의 독약을 매매하고 다니는 이상, 아무도 진실을 진실이라고 감히 말하지 않을 것입니다.

그러므로 자식이 아비를 불신하고, 에미는 지아비의 방탕에 할말을 잃고, 형제는 인신매매를 저주하려 나서지 않을 것입니다. 마침내 이 땅은 노예와 비겁한 자들의 지옥으로 변하고 말 것입니다. (신경질적으로 웃고 난 다음)

그러나… 하늘이 열리는 날, 저 하늘이 활짝 열리는 그 날은 반드시 오고야 맙니다. 인간을 초월하는 그 분이 오시는 날, 여러분은 어느 쪽에 서겠습니까? 그 분의 오른쪽입니까? 왼쪽입니까? 축복의 대열에 끼일 것입니까? 아니면, 저주받은 영원한 악마의 무리에 섞여서 고개를 수그릴 것입니까? (객석을 향해 손가락질을 하며)

거기에 중립은 없습니다. 우물쭈물 망설이면서 어설프게 신중론을 떠들어대던 무리는 유

neutrality. Hesitate day after day. Preach your discretion first wisdom. How childish! You will slowly sink in the lake of sulphur fire. How about the people who live holding the Tower of Babel on their head? How about the slaves who, buried in the Tower's ruins, cannot freely breathe, even for a moment during their whole life? As long as they are unable to discover their real freedom, they will never embrace the moment of salvation, until their mouths are infested by maggots. No, the salvation will never come back here, until they see the eternal moment when their names are recorded in the terrible book *(pause)*. Then, watch this small stage. Very closely. Here is nothing, but everything is here. You can't see anything here, but this is lacking nothing. The time to choose is given only once to each one... Now is the period of time you can't waste away...

(While she dances, and is enchanted to the noisy sound of a gong, a flute, a drum, a can, a log and a iron bar, the lights quikly go out.)

황불의 연못으로 천천히 가라앉을 것입니다. 머리 위에 바벨탑을 이고 사는 자들, 그 폐허 아래 깔려 숨 한번 자유로이 쉬지 못하고 사는 노예들, 진정 자유를 발견하지 못하는 이상, 그들은 입에서 구더기가 득시글거릴 때까지 단 한번도 구원의 순간을 포옹하지 못할 것입니다. 아니, 그들 이름이 저 참혹한 책에 기록되는 영원의 순간에 이르기까지 구원은 결코 돌아오지 않을 것입니다. (사이)

그러면 이제 이 작은 무대를 보십시오! 아무것도 없으나 모든 것이 있고, 모든 것이 보이지 않아도 아무것도 궁핍하지 않은 이 무대를 말입니다! 선택의 시간은 각자에게 단 한 번만 주어지는 것… 지금은 낭비할 시간이 아닙니다.

꽹과리, 피리, 북, 깡통, 통나무, 철봉 등이 내는 불협화음에 맞추어 여인이 신들린 듯 춤을 출 때 조명이 나간다.

Act One

living room of a Catholic priest, Seoul

The lights in again. A living room of a Catholic priest. On the left side of the stage we can see a small desk and a chair, and on the right, a bookshelf. Between the bookshelf and the audience an exit door leads to the outside. A crucifix and a radio are on the desk. Sitting on the chair, a young Catholic priest, in his thirties, is reading a weekly magazine, quite sensational and sensual. As he turns on the radio stretching an arm, a popsong's tune flows.

Priest *(clears his throat)* Ahem! Ahem! Hm... *(browses the weekly)* Eh? They have caught an illegal gambling group playing on a million dollar scale? Wow! This is quite wonderful. But... How was it possible they had such a tremendous sum of money? *(pause)* The top of

제1장

서울 시내 어느 본당신부의 응접실

조명이 다시 들어오면 신부의 응접실이 드러난다. 무대 왼쪽에 작은 책상과 걸상이, 오른쪽에 서가가 보인다. 서가와 객석 사이가 밖으로 통하는 출입문이고, 책상에는 십자가와 라디오가 놓여 있다. 의자에 앉아서 주간지를 읽던 신부가 팔을 뻗어 라디오를 틀면 대중가요 가락이 흐른다.

신부 (헛기침을 한다) 흐흠… (주간지를 뒤적이며) 억대 도박단 사건이라… 거 굉장한데? 그 많은 돈이 어디서 나왔을까? (사이)
"그대와 부르는 블루스"가 금주 인기가요 제

this week is a song titled "A blues I sing with you"... *(He crosses his legs. Someone knocks on the door very cautiously. He quickly puts the weekly in a drawer and picks up the Bible. He stands up turning the radio dial. Now we can hear classical music. He pretends to read the Bible.)* The door is open! Come in, please.

He stands with his back against the bookshelf. A Catholic Sister, seemingly 40-year old, opens the door and enters. She bows politely to him.

Sister Praised be Jesus, Mary and Joseph!

Priest Ah, yes... Come in, Sister.

Sister Sorry to disturb you, Father, in particular reading the Holy Bible.

Priest *(benevolently smiling)* Disturb me? No, not at all. Because Jesus had never disliked the people coming to him, whatever their number was... Something goes wrong again in your nunnery, I suppose?

Sister *(quite embarrassed)* Nothing wrong... No, it's not that...*(Seemingly hesitates)*

1위라…

(다리를 포개어 앉는다. 문 두드리는 소리가 조심스럽다. 신부가 재빨리 주간지를 책상 서랍에 집어넣은 뒤 성경책을 집어 든다. 일어서서 라디오의 다이얼을 돌리면 고전음악이 들린다. 성경을 펴서 읽는 척하며) 네에! 들어오십시오. (책상을 등지고 선다)

수녀 (문을 열고 들어서서 공손히 절을 하며) 찬미 예수, 마리아, 요셉!

신부 아, 수녀님이시군.

수녀 성경을 읽으시는 데 방해가 되어서 죄송합니다, 신부님.

신부 (너그럽게 미소하며) 아니, 방해될 건 없어요. 예수님께서도 찾아오는 군중을 싫어한 적이 없으니까… 그런데 수녀원에 또 무슨 일이라도 있었나요…?

수녀 (당황해 하며) 그…그런 게 아니라… 저… (망설이는 눈치다)

Priest *(in tender voice)* Tell me, Sister. The more difficult the problems are, the more ready I am to hear.

Sister *(hesitating, as if she wished to turn back to the door)* I'd better tell her to come again some other day.

Priest *(pretending to be surprised)* Some other day? Is someone waiting for me out there?

Sister Yes, Father. Miss Hong Young-ja, living on New Wave Street... *(in irritated voice)* I don't know why she did not inform me in advance...

Priest *(abruptly changing his attitude, becoming very stiff and formal)* What is her Christian name?

Sister Magdalene, Father.

Priest *(as if reminded then)* Ah, Magdalene! She is a bar hostess, isn't she? What's the matter with her?

Sister She wishes to do a confession.

Priest Aha, confession...Now? *(pause)* Well, it's not good time for me to hear confessions... *(pause)* Her house is not far from the church, I know. Tell her to come tomorrow. Yes, tomorrow is Saturday. Sister, will you remind her that every Saturday I hear confessions in the church from

신부 (부드러운 음성으로) 말씀하세요, 수녀님. 어려운 일일수록 내겐 어울리니까요.

수녀 (문쪽으로 돌아서려는 듯 망설이며) 아무래도 다음에 오라고 해야겠어요.

신부 (놀란 듯) 다음에 오다니? 밖에 누가 와 있습니까?

수녀 신파동에 사는 홍영자라는 여인이… (짜증기가 섞인 음성으로) 미리 연락이나 했어야지, 원….

신부 (사무적인 태도로 급히 변하며) 세례명이 뭐라고 했더라…

수녀 막달레나입니다.

신부 (그제서야 생각이 난 듯) 아, 홍막달레나? 거… 술집에 나가는 여자 말이군. 그래서요?

수녀 고백성사를 보겠다는데…

신부 아하, 그래…요? (사이) 그렇지만 지금은 좀 곤란한데… (사이) 그 여자 집이 성당에서 가까울 테니까 내일 오라고 해요. 내일은 토요일, 오후 4시부터 6시까지 성당에서 고백성사

4 to 6 p.m.? *(aside)* Good heavens! How can a sheep of my parish be so ignorant of regular time of confession?

Sister I will, but...

Priest Sister can explain well to her, I believe. Any reason you can advance to send her back.

Sister *(tries to protest in some way, but eventually resigns herself)* I think I really disturbed your precious time of quiet meditation. *(bowing)* Praised be Jesus, Our Lord. *(turns around)*

Priest *(sitting on the desk)* Praised be Jesus. Well, it's like... *(Sister turns to the Priest)* How much money is there collected in the box of atonement? Plenty enough, I should believe?

Sister *(calmly)* I'm afraid not so, because nowadays not so many people come to visit the church. As you know, Father, almost all the people here are poor.

Priest Aha, poor! That's the very point, and the problem, too. To be poor is natural, but it can't be any excuse. They are miserly in offerings to the church, because they are not ready to repent of their sins. They seldom repent, all

를 준다고 알려주시죠, 수녀님. (혼잣말처럼) 그것 참! 신자라면 고백성사 시간쯤 알고 있을 텐데….

수녀 네, 그러나…

신부 수녀님이 잘 말해서 돌려보내세요.

수녀 (뭔가 항의하려다가 말고 단념한 듯) 조용한 묵상시간에 공연히 번거롭게 해드린 것 같군요. (절하며) 찬미 예수. (돌아선다)

신부 (책상에 걸터앉으며) 찬미 예수. 그런데, 참… (수녀가 돌아선다) 속죄함에 헌금은 많이 모였겠지요?

수녀 (담담하게) 요즘은 성당을 찾아오는 사람이 별로 없어서…, 그리고 우리 성당 구역에는 가난한 사람들만 살기 때문에…

신부 하아, 문제는 바로 거기에 있는 거예요. 그건 가난에다 탓을 돌릴 문제가 아니지요. 사람들이 도무지 철면피처럼 뉘우칠 줄을 모르니까 헌금에 인색한 겁니다. 아, 거 홍막달레나에게도 우선 헌금을 권유해 보세요. 헌금

the shameless ones. Well, why don't you Sister advise the girl...Miss Hong, you said?

Sister What shall I advise?

Priest Putting some money into the box before she does a confession. An offering is also a sign to repent whole-heartedly, you know better than me, Sister. *(doubtful and absent-minded, she just looks at him)* And tell the kitchen maid to prepare a roasted chicken for me this evening.

Sister Now I remember. The kitchen maid wanted me to tell you... if you can raise her monthly salary. Just a little more. She has to send the money to her parents in her hometown, Father.

Priest *(suddenly bursting into anger)* Raise the salary? Always the same story again? When you work for the church, you should not be blinded by the greedy desire for money. If she is stubborn and will not understand this principle, pound it into her bird's head, Sister. When participating in the holy works of God, everyone has to stick to the spirit of sacrifice. Salary...hm... Such a trivial matter can be smoothed by you, Sister.

이란 자기 죄를 진정으로 뉘우친다는 징표도 되니까. (수녀가 의아한 표정으로 신부를 멍하니 쳐다본다.)

그리고 주방에다는 통닭을 한 마리 준비하도록 일러 주고…

수녀 참, 식모애가 월급을 올려달라고 하던데요, 신부님. 고향에 계시는 부모님께 송금한다면서요.

신부 (갑자기 화를 내며) 월급타령을 또 한다? 교회를 위해서 일하는 사람들이 너무 돈에만 욕심을 내면 안 된다고 잘 타일러 주시오. 하느님의 사업에 참여한다면 희생정신이 있어야지. 그런 문제는 수녀님이 잘 처리할 줄 믿겠습니다.

Sister Principle is good, I know. Sacrifice... Well, however... She is receiving too small amount, I think. Hardly more than 50 dollars. *(surprised by her own words)* Father, my intention is not to...

Priest *(raising his tone)* If it is heard by someone... *(clears his voice)* Huh huh! They may accuse us like... cutting a kitchen maid's salary, the church is exploiting her.

Sister *(more embarrassed)* I didn't mean it that way...

Priest I never doubt your real intention, Sister. Now, well...

Sister I'll tell her your views. *(turns her back and exits)*

Priest *(aside)* Look at how people behave these days! *(shaking his head from left to right)* They have no spirit of sacrifice at all. This is the most serious problem. No one is willing to do their service for Jesus, but everyone demands only the miracle to multiply the bread. My God! Do they think I were a Jesus?

(closing the Bible, he puts it on the desk. And he takes again the popular weekly out of the drawer and opens it. When he turns the radio dial, a pop song tune

수녀 아무리 그래도… 보수가 너무 적은 것 같아요. 한 달에 겨우 2천 원… (당황해 하며) 저, 이건 그냥…

신부 (언성을 높이며) 누가 들으면… (헛기침을 한다) 허허, 교회가 식모애 월급을 깎아서 착취한다고 하겠습니다.

수녀 (더욱 당황해지며) 제 말은 그런 뜻이 아니고 그저…

신부 알아요, 알아. 자, 이제…

수녀 신부님 말씀대로 전하죠. (돌아서서 나간다)

신부 (혼잣말로) 요새 사람들은 (고개를 좌우로 흔들며) 희생정신이 없어서 탈이란 말이야. 예수님을 위해서 봉사할 생각은 않고 빵을 불리는 기적만 자꾸 요구하고 있으니, 나 원… 내가 어디 예순가?

(성경을 덮어 책상 위에 놓고 서랍에서 주간지를 다시 꺼내 펴 든다. 라디오의 다이얼을 돌리면 대중가요가 흐른다. 사이)

신부라고 해서 사회를 모르면 안 되지. 뭐, 이

flows. Pause.)

A Priest, too, has to l know about the society he lives in. This weekly? Too sensational? Well... I'm not reading it just for fun. This is rather a textbook of my social analysis. How useful! I'm now studying. And that, very hardly. If I know nothing about how much our society is corrupted and how serious its illness is, then, I'll never be a good and able pastor. Hm... Of course, this is quite interesting. I enjoy it, well, maybe more than I think. However, strictly speaking, this is my social study.

(As soon as he starls to read the weekly sitting on the chair, someone knocks on the door again. He quickly puts it in the drawer, takes up the Bible and turns off the radio.)

SISTER *(re-enters)* Praised be Jesus, Mary, Joseph. I'm deeply sorry, Father. I really don't want to disturb your Bible reading again.

PRIEST *(in an unfriendly tone)* The bar hostess hasn't gone back yet? *(bares frankly his feeling annoyed)*

SISTER It's not her, but...

PRIEST Another matter, then?

거? 이건 재미삼아 보는 게 아니라 사회 분석 교과서로 읽는 거니까 괜찮아. 공부지, 공부. 세상이 얼마나 썩고 병들었는지 모르고 앉아 있다고 해서 훌륭한 신부는 아니거든. 음, 물론 약간의 재미가 없는 건 아니지. 하지만 이건 어디까지나 사회 연구야.

(의자에 앉아서 주간지를 뒤적이려고 할 때 다시 문 두드리는 소리가 들린다. 재빠르게 주간지를 서랍에 집어넣고 성경을 든 뒤 라디오를 끈다.)

수녀 (들어서며) 찬미 예수, 마리아, 요셉. 신부님, 너무 죄송합니다. 성경 읽으시는데 자꾸만 방해를 해서요.

신부 (퉁명스럽게) 술집 여잔 아직도 안 갔소? (몹시 귀찮아하는 기색이 뚜렷하다)

수녀 그게 아니라…

신부 그럼?

Sister Chairman Kim sent a man.

Priest *(in a kind tone, and expectantly)* Which Chairman Kim? Is he the owner of a big textile company?

Sister A pharmaceutical company, he said.

Priest *(very glad to hear that news)* Oh! It's Chairman Paul Kim. Why did he send for me?

Sister Today is the first anniversary of his youngest son's birthday, the messenger said. Chairman Kim wishes you to be present in the party at his house.

Priest When is the party to start?

Sister At seven, he said. *(looks at her wristwatch)*

Priest *(looking at his wristwatch)* Only one hour from the party! *(to her)* Tell him I'll be there soon. Now, what kind of present shall I prepare for his son?

Sister Your blessing will be more than enough, he said, Father.

Priest *(aside)* A priest has the power to bless, but no money for a present. They seem to know it so well. How smart a people! *(to her)* Then, it's all right. Tell the kitchen maid she doesn't need to prepare the dinner table any more.

수녀 김사장 댁에서 사람이 찾아왔습니다.

신부 (은근하게) 어느 김사장? 방직회사 김사장 말인가?

수녀 제약회사라던데요?

신부 (반색하며) 아, 김바오로 사장이군. 그래서?

수녀 막내아들 돌이 오늘인데 신부님을 꼭 모시고 싶답니다.

신부 몇 시라죠?

수녀 일곱 시라던데요. (시계를 본다)

신부 (팔목시계를 보며) 한 시간밖에 안 남았군. (수녀에게) 가겠다고 전해요. 그런데 선물은 뭘루 한다?

수녀 그냥 오셔서 축복해 달라던데요.

신부 (혼잣말로) 신부에게 축복의 능력은 있어도 선물 살 돈은 없다는 걸 아는 모양이군. (수녀에게) 알았습니다. 주방에 저녁 준비는 필요 없다고 해 주시오.

Sister The table will be perfect, except a roasted chicken.

Priest A roasted chicken?

Sister She needs a dinner, too.

Priest Oh, yes... of course. *(She goes out of the door. Pause. He speaks aside)* Did she say Chairman Paul Kim? He is always very generous. He donated unsparingly, once again, when the bronze statue of Jesus was erected in the front yard of my church. Hm... No doubt he will be a great donor as before. *(looking at his wristwatch)* I have still a lot of time before leaving here. Fifteen minutes will be enough to get to his house. *(After putting down the Bible on the desk, he takes the weekly again and turns on the radio. An emotional pop song flows.)* Ha! What's this? A confession of a certain actress... *(pause)*

While he smiles very broadly with a nod, the lights go out.

수녀 통닭만 빼면 되겠습니다.

신부 통닭?

수녀 식모애도 밥은 먹어야죠.

신부 아, 그렇겠군. (수녀가 문으로 나간다. 사이. 혼잣말로) 김사장이라…, 지난번 청동으로 예수님 동상을 세울 때도 그 사람의 힘이 컸지. 흠, 앞으로도 우리 교회에 많은 도움을 줄 인물이야. (시계를 보며) 시간은 아직 충분해. 가는데 15분이면 되니까. (성경을 책상위에 놓고 서랍에서 다시 주간지를 꺼내 들고 라디오를 켠다. 대중가요 가락이 흐른다) 어느 여배우의 고백이라…. (사이)

신부가 싱긋이 미소하며 고개를 끄떡일 때 조명이 나간다.

Act Two

front street at the entrance of a Catholic church

The street at the church's entrance. With their backs to a red brick wall, a leper and a beggar squat on the ground, distanced a little from each other. Each has an empty can before him.

Beggar *(in a hilarious tone, like singing a folklore song)* Oh, no, no, no, don't try to talk me off! No use talking anymore! Now, I'm entering. I'm entering. *(aside)* Entering what? Between the thighs? Ha! *(sighs deeply, warming his hands with his breath, impatiently)* Damn it! What a cold today! Hey, you dirty leper! Collected some bucks?

Leper Not even a dog's ball. How about you, the most God-forsaken beggar?

제2장

성당 입구 앞길

성당 입구의 길. 벽돌담을 등지고 문둥이와 거지가 쭈그리고 앉아 있다. 깡통을 하나씩 앞에 놓았다.

거지 (민요를 부르듯 신이 나서) 아니, 글쎄, 그러지 말아. 입 닥쳐. 닥치라구. 에, 씨구씨구 들어간다. (혼잣말로) 어디로 들어가? 가랭이 사이로? 흥! (한숨 쉬듯 두 손을 호호 불며) 어 추워, 염병할! 야, 문둥아! 좀 벌었냐?

문둥이 개부랄도 없다. 염병할 거지 넌?

Beggar Me, too. Not even something similar to a dog's ball had fallen in my can. Bullshit people! All of them should die of smallpox or pestilence. How could I get a buck or a coin when no shadow passed in front of me? I don't mind the shadows, living or dead, but they are now playing with girls. Drinking? Of course!

Leper *(pretending good manners)* Shut up! Why shouldn't they do that in such a cold, and evening? *(pause)*

Beggar So sharp a cold to you?

Leper It makes me crazy. *(pause)* How about making a fire?

Beggar Have any?

Leper Two.

Beggar Show me.

Leper *(Fumbles in his pocket with a rustling sound and, a moment later, takes out of it two stubs of cigarette. He says very proudly)* Look, what do you say? You can get nothing better than these, nowhere. No agree? These really are the best.

거지 난 개부랄 비슷한 것도 없다. 지랄 염병, 빌어먹다 꼬꾸라질 새끼들이 어디 지나가야 해먹지. 계집 끼고 술이나 처먹고 있으니 그림자도 안 보여.

문둥이 (점잖빼며) 임마, 추울 땐 그러는 거야. (사이)

거지 추워?

문둥이 그래. (사이) 장작 땔까?

거지 있냐?

문둥이 두 개.

거지 어디?

문둥이 (주머니를 부스럭대며 뒤지다 담배꽁초 두 개를 꺼낸다. 자랑스러운 듯) 어때? 이만하면 극상품이지? 이런 건 아무데서도 못 구하는 거야.

Beggar The best? Ha! Incurable stonehead you are. I could have found the longer one if I had tried. Anyway, a fox had thrown them, surely, I think.

Leper Where is a fox on this street?

Beggar I mean a lady with nothing to do. She has but time and money to spend stupidly.

Leper No, it's not that kind. A cicada did.

Beggar You say a cicada?

Leper Got no idea?

Beggar Not a bit of dust.

Leper Lick your boots.

Beggar I've no boots.

Leper Then, your filthy feet.

Beggar My tongue will be unhappy.

Leper I don't mind. How dare you teach me a fox when you don't know a cicada? A cicada means... a bar hostess.

Beggar What's the difference between them? Nothing. Both of them are buckets of muddy water. Better for them to shit into a deformed, rusted dustbin. I can't tell one from the other when each is robbing a purse of an idiot, fool

거지 죽어도 더럽게 쬐그만 거 죽었구나? 여우가 피우던 거겠지.

문둥이 여우?

거지 유한마담 말야. 몰라?

문둥이 아냐, 매미야.

거지 매미?

문둥이 몰라?

거지 뭔데?

문둥이 빌어먹을 놈! 여우는 알면서 매민 몰라? 술집에서 노는 기집 말야.

거지 그게 그거 아냐. 꾸정물통이야 다 같지. 찌그러진 깡통에다가 똥쌀 년들. 얼간이 병신들 주머니 터는 덴 다 마찬가지라구. 커피 한 잔 값이면 나 같은 놈 이틀은 살것다. (민요를 부르듯 신이 나서)에라, 빌어먹을 씨구씨구. 자, 하나 줘, 이 문둥아.

and gentleman all at once. If I were given coins just for a cup of coffee, I could live on it, at least for two days. Damn it! *(in a joyful tone, like singing a folklore song)* Oh, no, no, no, don't curse me off! Now, I'm entering. Hey, you bad smelling leper! Give me one of them quickly.

Leper Oh, you impossible beggar! How clean and beautiful you are! Here goes it. *(throws a stub of cigarette to the beggar. Pause)* Wait a minute! No problem, if we enjoy a smoke here?

Beggar *(stops his gesture to strike a match)* You are so smart and wise. If we smoke, our business will go up in smoke, too. Because those damned devils don't think we are the same human beings as they are. Therefore, if we make a fire on the stub, those sons of a bitch will laugh just passing away. No buck, no coin to us. To them we are too ridiculous. We have to pay, they say, the price of our haughtiness to imitate their smoking hobby. *(to the audience)* Oh, you sons of a bitch filthier than any kind of excrement! Oh, this damned stench! You care for your own fowl smell! *(With a comical gesture he puts*

문둥이 옛따, 이 거지새끼야. (꽁초를 거지에게 준다. 사이) 잠깐! 이 장작 여기서 때도 될까?

거지 (성냥을 켜려다 말고) 옳거니! 장사 안 돼. 우라질 새끼들은 우릴 사람으로 안 보거든. 그러니까 우리가 이 장작을 때면 그 새끼들은 웃고 지나간다구. 가소롭다 이거지. 지들 하는 거 건방지게 흉내내지 말라 이거지. (관객을 향해) 야, 이 똥물에 튀길 놈의 새끼들아! 더럽다, 더러워! (성냥과 꽁초를 주머니에 집어넣는다. 문둥이도 꽁초를 자기 주머니에 넣는다) 야, 문둥아, 큰길로 나가자.

the match and the stub in his pocket. The leper does likewise following him exactly) Hey, you damned leper, my fellow traveller! Let's go to a main street.

LEPER Did I hear main street? Is your brain normal as before? No!

BEGGAR Why not? What the hell do you mean by that no?

LEPER They'll take us away! Arrested, you know.

BEGGAR Afraid of street gentlemen in their black clothes? Well, if they wish, let them take us away. Prison? Damn the prison! In these damned streets of Seoul, why shouldn't we beg our bread? We are not granted even the very freedom of begging? Even a small piece of bread for our empty belly? Who did authorize them to grant us such a freedom or not? We have to live until we die. Then, we must eat. Did the heaven open our mouths simply as decorations of our body? Gosh! If they will, let them arrest us as they wish! A prison is rather better than here to us. Even if should die there in prison, it's more welcome than to die frozen on the street.

문둥이 큰길? 안 돼.

거지 안 되긴 뭐가 안 된다는 거야?

문둥이 잡혀 가잖아!

거지 거 새카만 옷 입은 나리들 땜에? 아, 뭐 잡아 갈 테면 잡아가라지. 감옥? 빌어먹을! 아니, 염병할 이놈의 서울바닥에선 비럭질도 마음대로 못한단 말야? 비럭질을 해서라도 목구멍에 풀칠할 자유마저 없다 이거야? 우리도 사람이니 처먹어야 살지. 아가린 폼으로 뚫어놨나? 헹, 잡아가려면 얼마든지 잡아가라고 해! 여기보단 차라리 빵깐이 낫다구. 뒈지더라도 거기가 낫지 뭘.

Leper Bravo! Every word is holy and true as the sayings of Confucius. In the prison, food is free, therefore, a coffin is free, too. *(pause)* No feeling cold?

Beggar Of course, I do. Almost frozen to death.

Leper I'm already a dead body. *(pause)* Some more bucks, let's get away from here. To survive such a terrible cold, at least, a cup of strong liquor is a must for us.

Beggar *(putting his finger on the lips)* Shht! A rabbit is coming down there.

From the left the Priest enters folding his arms. He holds the Bible under one of his arms.

Priest *(aside)* Perhaps, I keep too close intimacy only with the rich people, don't I? Too much interested in my parishioners' offerings, regular and special, I neglect the poor people, don't I? I do judge the weight of a soul by his clothes, don't I? *(pause)* No, well... Perhaps, yes... I have no choice to make my church's affairs well done. How can I manage my parish

문둥이 구구 절절 공자 말씀이다. 콩밥은 공짜니까. 관도 공짜지. (사이) 춥지 않냐?

거지 왜 안 추워? 송장이 다 되어 가는데….

문둥이 난 벌써 송장이야. (사이) 한 장만 채우면 일어나자. 쐬주라도 칵 한잔 불어야 살것다.

거지 쐬주? 거 좋오치. 벌써부터 군침 돌아 미치것다.

문둥이 (손가락을 입에 대고) 쉬잇! 하나 굴러 온다.

무대 왼쪽에서 신부가 팔짱을 낀 채 걸어 들어온다. 성경을 옆구리에 꼈다.

신부 (혼잣말로) 내가 너무 부자들 하고만 친하게 지내는 게 아닐까? 교무금이나 특별헌금에 지나치게 관심을 두고, 가난한 사람들을 소홀히 대하는 건 아닐까? 입은 옷만 보고 그 사람의 영혼의 경중을 판단하는 건 아닐까? (사이) 아냐, 그래야 일이 되는 걸? 가난한 신자들만 가지고는 교회 운영이 될 턱이 없지. 아냐, 사

well enough only with the poor? Impossible. Am I an exceptional case in these matters? The other pastors are all the same as myself. In these days all of us follow exactly the same pattern. Poverty! Poverty! Let's love the poverty! Even though I alone preach like that, it's useless. As a result, I alone, will be isolated, left out in the cold. All of them will laugh at me saying I'm an idiot. But... *(pause)* Ah, why do I lack the courage so miserably? The true path of a pastor is... No, it's not... I'd recover my strength. All said and done, the reality is here beyond my power to change it.

BEGGAR Oh, no, no, no, please, don't turn your face about. Now, I'm entering. I'm entering. I keep on living, cause I have no courage to cut it off. I'll thank you millions of times even for a graceful shadow of a coin. Have mercy on me, please. *(prostrates flat)*

LEPER *(following the beggar's gesture)* I'm just one of the poor, miserable people, Your Excellency.

PRIEST *(seemingly deeply moved)* Oh, dear brothers of Jesus! *(comes nearer as if to embrace them, but*

실 뭐 나만 그런가? 다른 신부들도 다 마찬가지야. 요새는 다 그래. 가난! 가난! 가난을 사랑합시다! 혼자서 공연히 떠들어 봤자 나만 고립돼. 따돌림 받지. 모두 비웃을 거야, 바보라고. 그러나… (사이) 아, 난 왜 이렇게 용기가 없을까? 올바른 성직의 길이란… 아냐, 힘을 내야지. 어디까지나 현실은 현실이야.

거지 에헤… 씨구씨구 들어간다. 죽지 못해 붙어 있는 목숨, 쐬푼 한닢이 그립습니다요. 에, 한 푼 줍쇼. (넙죽 엎드린다)

문둥이 (따라 엎드리며) 불쌍한 백성입니다요, 나리.

신부 (감동한 듯) 오오, 예수님의 형제들이여! (껴안기라도 할 듯 가까이 다가가다가 갑자기 멈추고 몸을 돌린다. 손으로 코를 막으며 혼잣말로) 아이구 이 냄새! 고기덩이, 뼈다귀 모조리 썩어 문드러지는 냄새야! (손을 내저으며) 휘이 휘이!

abruptly stops and turns his back against them. Covering his nose, he says aside) Ouch! What the hellish smell! Like all the flesh, all the bones are decaying and collapsing! *(waving his other hand violently)* Away this smell! Away!

Leper *(rubbing his hands continuously)* A sick and poor fellow I am, Sir. Too much cold and hungry that I beg Your Excellency so eagerly. Have you ever seen anyone ill who was willing to get ill? Otherwise, did anyone insist to remain a cripple, because he didn't wish to be cured? Lacking money makes anyone a wretch cripple, lacking money condemns him guilty, Sir. Have mercy to grant me some coins, please.

Priest I'm not an Excellency, nor a government official. *(covering his nose again)* This smell kills me!

Beggar *(raises his head)* Considering the thick book under your arm, your excellency looks like you belong to the higher rank that rules over our lives less worthy than a fly's. Oh, no, no, no, don't talk me off. Our lives are just like floating around plants, therefore, no money, therefore,

문둥이 (두 손을 비비며) 병든 놈입니다요. 춥고 배고파 이렇게 싹싹 빕니다요, 나리. 어느 놈 병들고 싶어 병들고, 병 고치기 싫어서 병신 신세 고집합니까요? 돈 없으면 병신이요, 돈 없는 게 죄지요. 나리, 한푼 줍쇼.

신부 난 나리가 아니오. (코를 막으며) 아이고, 이 냄새!

거지 (고개를 들고) 두툼한 책을 옆구리에 낀 걸 보니 나리는 우리 같은 파리 목숨을 다스리는 지체 높은 어른 같습니다요. 에헤야, 우리 같은 부초 인생은 돈 없으니 계집질은 생각도 못하고, 배운 게 없으니 사기 칠 수도 없고…

we dare not even imagine the running after women. And we have no learning, therefore, we don't know how to cheat the others.

Leper *(also raises his head and gazes at the Priest's face)* Not qualified to keep an entry in the 'Who's Who', therefore, I'm a rubbish unable to take a bribe like the others. Pity on a dayfly's life and toss me some coins.

Priest *(unfolds his arms and looks at the wristwatch)* If I do not hurry, I'll be late. *(to the beggar)* I'm terribly busy, now. See you later.

Beggar *(grubs the lower edges of the Priest's trousers)* To a wretched beggar there is no tomorrow, no later. Your Excellency! Whenever you see a beggar, he is simply a beggar. Mercy to grant me some coins.

Leper *(aside to the audience)* He looks like a Catholic priest. But, what a miser he is!

Priest *(to the beggar)* You look quite learned.

Beggar *(laughing disgustingly)* Hee, hee, hee! Once upon a time my story was different from now. I was the president of my class, of course, in the elementary school. President! Hee, hee, hee!

문둥이 (고개를 들어 신부를 빤히 쳐다보며) 유명인사도 아니니 뇌물도 못 받아먹는 쓰레기, 하루살이 목숨 어여삐 여기시어 한푼만 적선합쇼.

신부 (팔짱을 풀고 손목시계를 보며) 이거 늦겠는걸? (거지에게) 난 바빠요. 나중에 다시 봅시다.

거지 (신부에게 매달리며) 빌어먹는 놈에겐 앞날이란 게 없습니다요. 나리! 언제 봐도 거지는 거지죠. 한푼만 줍쇼.

문둥이 (혼잣말로 객석을 향해) 이거 신부인 모양인데 더럽게 짱아로 노네.

신부 (거지에게) 넌 제법 유식하구나?

거지 (징그럽게 웃으며) 헤헤헤, 이래 뵈도 초등학교 땐 반장도 했습죠. 헤헤헤.

Priest *(aside)* Ouch! What a smell! It really kills me. This beggar had never brushed the teeth since his birth till now. *(looking at the leper, he is surprised)* My God! This is a leper.
If not cautious enough, I may risk infection. Oh, leprosy in the street! *(to the beggar)* Then, you are not a beggar by birth? Well, of course... No man is wicked from the birth. As Jesus Christ already said...

Beggar There are so numerous people who die as beggars. Oh, no, no, no, don't talk me off. I'm entering. I'm entering your...

Leper Who is this Jesus Christ, Your Excellency? Hee, hee, hee! *(aside to the audience)*. This fellow is surely a Christian by name only. Always preaching, but not practising!

Priest *(prays aside)* My Lord of love! Make your priests full of your mercy and let them, in turn, feed always plentifully the people in this land with the words of salvation. *(to the beggar and leper in a solemn tone)* Jesus is Our Lord who loves, the most ardently, people like you—the sick, the weak and the abandoned. Whenever he

신부 (혼잣말로) 원, 무슨 냄새가 이렇게 지독할까? 양치질이라곤 태어나서부터 지금까지 한 번도 안한 거지로군. (문둥이를 보고 놀라며) 아니, 이건 문둥이잖아? 까딱하면 전염될라. 조심해야지. (거지에게) 날 때부터 거지는 아니었다 이거지? 그래, 사람은 날 때부터 나쁘진 않아요. 예수님께서도 말씀했지만…

거지 죽을 때 거지되는 사람은 많습니다요. 데헤야, 얼씨구 들어간다.

문둥이 예수가 뉘신가요, 나리? 헤헤헤헤. (혼잣말로 객석을 향해) 이놈도 예수쟁이가 틀림 없어. 주둥아리만 발랑 까진 쟁이….

신부 (혼잣말로 기도한다) 사랑의 주님! 성직자들이 동정심에 가득차서 이 땅의 백성들을 구원의 말씀으로 항상 배불리 먹이게 하소서. (거지와 문둥이에게 엄숙한 어조로) 예수님은 당신네처럼 병들고 약하고 버림받은 사람들을 가장 사랑하는 분이요. 이렇게 추운 길거리에서 굶주림에 시달리고 외로움에 찌든 거지나 문둥이

meets a beggar or a leper on the street who, stricken by loneliness, suffers hunger, he always sheds abundant tears for them. Jesus is such a merciful Lord. *(aside)* Why do I preach to them now? What consolation can my words give them? *(looking again at the wristwatch)* If I continue, surely I'll be late. I had to pretend not to see them and just pass.

LEPER *(arises)* Your Excellency knows this man called Jesus very well? What kind of relation do you have with him?

PRIEST *(aside)* The longer I stay here, the more annoying questions they just raise. *(to both of them)* I'm the main priest of this Catholic church. If you wish to know about Jesus, come later and learn. Now I'm terribly busy because of my appointment, I have to hurry. Excuse me.

BEGGAR *(suddenly raising his body, he stands in the Priest's way)* If you are truly the main priest, sir, show me the mercy of some bucks or coins before you leave here. If the man called Jesus happened to come this way, he might have given me a lot of money, might he not? Oh, no,

를 보면 눈물을 펑펑 쏟으시는 분이 바로 예수님이요. (혼잣말로) 내 말이 이것들에게 무슨 위로가 된다고 지껄이는 걸까? (다시 손목시계를 보며) 이러다간 정말 늦겠는 걸? 모른 척하고 그냥 지나갈 걸 잘못했어.

문둥이 (일어서며) 나리는 거 예수란 사람 잘 아슈? 어떤 관계시죠?

신부 (혼잣말로) 이거 자꾸만 귀찮은 질문만 던지는군. (거지와 문둥이에게) 난 저 성당의 주임 신부요. 예수님을 알고 싶거든 나중에 성당에 와서 배우도록 하시오. 나, 난 약속이 있어서 바쁘니까 이만….

거지 (벌떡 일어서서 신부의 앞길을 가로 막으며) 나리가 정말 신부라면 한푼 주고 가쇼. 예수란 사람이 여기 지나간다면 동냥도 푸짐하게 주지 않았겠습니까요. 에헤야, 씨구씨구 들어간다. 썩은 우거지 같은 가련한 이 몸. 밥 한술, 술찌게미 한 사발이 그립다. 자, 한푼만 적선합쇼. 사지가 얼어 들어오는뎁쇼.

no, on, don't talk me off. Now I'm entering. I'm entering. My body, so miserable as a rotten cabbage, is longing for a bowl of rice or a handful of residue after the rice wine. Now, some bucks or coins. My limbs grow colder, almost frozen numb.

Leper *(tries to catch the Priest's sleeves, but the Priest retreats)* If even this Jesus is the same as the wealthy people, I have no other option but to hate him. Why? Cause they always try to exploit anyone, even the lowest like us, as they like. Hee, hee, hee!

Priest Huh, huh, huh... Bless my soul! Jesus is not like that, but the Lord of truth and love. *(looking at his wristwatch)* I'm already late. Now, I should go quickly.

The Priest tries to go out to right, but the beggar and leper bar his way.

Beggar Some bucks!

Leper *(menacingly)* Just one buck, at least!

Priest *(waving his hand with the Bible)* Nothing, I have

문둥이 (신부의 소매를 붙잡으려 하면 신부가 피한다) 예수마저 저 부자 놈들 하고 똑같다면 전 싫습니다. 부자들은 우리 같은 놈마저 지네들 입맛대로 써 먹으려 덤벼들거든요. 헤헤헤헤.

신부 허허허, 나 이거 원… 예수님은 그런 분이 아니라 진실과 사랑의 주님이요. (시계를 보며) 정말 늦었군. 이젠 가야지.

신부가 오른쪽으로 나가려 한다. 거지와 문둥이가 가로 막는다

거지 한푼 줍쇼.

문둥이 (위협적으로) 딱 한푼만 줍쇼.

신부 (성경 든 손을 내저으며) 없어요, 없어. 난 돈이 없단 말이오. 주고 싶어도 돈이 있어야 주지…

nothing. No money with me. Even though I wish to give, how can I give you money that I have not?

Leper A lie!

Beggar Right. It's a lie!

Priest *(angrily)* What? How dare you say I'm lying?

Leper You have money, sir. And you are a Christian, trumpeting, sir. Ain't I right?

Priest *(hysterically)* My God! How rude you are! I said I had nothing to give. No one can give to anyone what he doesn't have with him. *(controls himself with great efforts)* That's the limit of any human being. Be a man ever endlessly merciful, but, if he has not a penny in his pocket, what's the use of his mercy? It is not even worthy to be proud of. Truly I say to you, I have not a penny with me. *(As if running away, he goes out to right.)*

Beggar The limit of any human being? Humph! *(spits on the ground)* Really stinking pig!

Leper Damned the rascal! No doubt a false Christian. The main priest of the church? What a

문둥이 거짓말이다!

거지 그래, 거짓말이야.

신부 (화가 나서) 뭐, 거짓말?

문둥이 나리는 돈이 있습죠. 그리고 예수쟁이죠? 그렇죠?

신부 (신경질적으로) 아니, 이것들이! 없다니까! 신부가 무슨 돈이 있다는 거요? 가지고 있지 않은 건 아무도 다른 사람에게 줄 수가 없는 거요. (애써 자제하며) 그게 인간의 한계라는 거요. 자비심이 아무리 많아도 주머니가 비면 무슨 소용이 있겠소? 자랑스럽지도 못한 거요. 난 정말 돈이 없단 말이오. (도망치듯 오른쪽으로 빠져나간다)

거지 인간의 한계? 흥! (땅에 침을 탁 뱉으며) 더러운 자식!

문둥이 빌어먹을! 저건 가짜 예수쟁이야. 신부? 돈 한 푼이 아까워 꽁무니를 빼다니 그게 무슨 꼴입니까요?

shameful scene he made, when he ran away so unwilling to give us even a penny!

Beggar *(in a singing tone of a folklore song)* Oh, no, no, no, don't talk me off. Damned the man! He vanished, already quickly vanished. An arrow missed the target, and the archer lost all his bearings. A bear with a wristwatch had really run away. My business collapsed. All is empty, all is useless. Darn it! Devil takes the beast!

Leper He is a friend of Jesus, and as poor as a beggar... Pew! Is he really poor? Of course, poor! As much as us! Then, how can I understand the irony, he has an expensive overcoat, wears wool shirts through the winter, and whenever invited, he can bite roasted ribs? Eh? What do you say? Oh, no, no, no, don't make me laugh! What the hell is this world where I cannot freely do even begging? Hey, you there! Now, I'm entering. I'm entering. Bull... What a cold!

The leper moves his body this or that way, as if trying to shake off the cold. Following the gesture, the beggar stamps his feet.

거지 (타령조로) 에에, 씨구씨구 나갔다. 날도 새고 틀렸다. 시계를 찬 곰새끼가 떠났다. 장사는 망했다. 말짱말짱 헛일이다. 에이, 염병할!

문둥이 예수하고 친하지만 거지처럼 가난하고… 흥, 가난하고… 가난해도 오바 입고, 털셔츠로 겨울 나고, 초대받으면 불갈비 뜯는 인간… 에헤야 절씨구… 빌어먹지도 못할 이놈의 세상! 어 씨구씨구. 어 추워.

문둥이가 추위를 떨쳐 버리기라도 하려는 듯 몸을 이리저리 움직인다. 거지도 따라서 발을 동동 구른다.

Beggar Why is this winter so terrible? Where did this God-damn cold come from?

Leper This is really murdering! Well, the devil... had better preached nothing before runaway. Damn the fellow! He just filled my balloon with hope to get a buck from him, but at last, darted off like a virgin girl exposed of her breaking wind. *(pause)*

Beggar But, you also belong to...

Leper To what? Whisky? Gambling? Debauchery? Such bad habits, I have nothing to do with them.

Beggar I mean, to the church.

Leper *(pretending)* Who do you mean to the church?

Beggar Here is no one except you.

Leper Why me?

Beggar Why not? When we met for the first time last evening, you said it.

Leper Did I? *(sighs)* Yes, I remember I did. Once I was... more than ten years ago.

Beggar Once? How about now?

Leper *(Sarcastically)* Now I am a leper. A leper more contemptuous than a dog which gnaws a bone

거지 무슨 겨울이 이다지 독하지?

문둥이 누가 아니래? 그런데… 지껄이지나 말고 꺼지지. 빌어먹을! 한푼 줄 듯 하다가 방귀 뀌다 들킨 처녀처럼 달아났어. (사이)

거지 참, 너 쟁이지?

문둥이 쟁이? 술쟁이, 도박쟁이, 오입쟁이? 그런 거나 인연 없어.

거지 예수쟁이 말야.

문둥이 (딴전부리며) 누가?

거지 너 말야.

문둥이 내가?

거지 그래, 어제 우리 처음 만났을 때 너 쟁이라고 했잖아?

문둥이 (한숨을 쉬며) 옛날에… 10년 전에.

거지 지금은 어때?

sitting at a Christian's door. A leper more stinking than the excrements of Christians, which are discharged as they like.

BEGGAR He said Jesus loves lepers, didn't he?

LEPER Jesus is Jesus, Christians are Christians, that's all. These stinking Christians are not Jesus.

BEGGAR *(thinks deep. Pause)* I can't see the difference at all.

LEPER It's too simple, you fish-head! The Jesus written of in the Holy Book is not the same as the Jesus trumpeted by these good, well, good-for-nothing Christians.

BEGGAR Then, there are many Jesus's you say?

LEPER *(face turns as red as a hot iron bar by sudden anger)* I don't care one or many. Don't you know the doctor who secretly hoarded medicines due to be distributed freely to lepers? Dr. Choi, the devil! Already reported by the newspapers. This filthy son of a bitch is Christian, too. He leaves his mouth in the church, but gives his hands to the king of devils. Small but quite a smart devil he is! He belongs simply to the kind of good-for-nothing Christians.

문둥이 (냉소적으로) 문둥이. 예수쟁이들 문간에 앉아서 빼다귀 뜯는 개새끼보다 더 천한 문둥이. 예수쟁이들이 싸갈기는 똥보다도 더 더러운 문둥이, 문둥이야.

거지 예수는 문둥이를 사랑한다면서?

문둥이 예수는 예수, 예수쟁이는 예수쟁이야. 예수쟁이는 예수가 아냐.

거지 (생각에 잠긴다. 사이) 뭐가 뭔지 난 모르겠다.

문둥이 성경책에 쓰여 진 예수하고 예수쟁이들이 떠벌여대는 예수는 같지 않다 이거야.

거지 어떻게?

문둥이 (악에 받친 듯) 문둥이한테 줄 약을 빼돌리는 의사, 알지? 최박사란 자식. 신문에 났지. 그 자식도 예수쟁이야. 입은 성당에 있지만 손은 악마와 악수하고 있는 놈이지. 번데기 같은 자식! 그런 자식은 그냥 쟁이야, 쟁이. 예수쟁이! 예수를 팔아먹는 예수쟁이란 말야.

Christians? Bah! How many of them are selling out Jesus, everyday? Like Dr. Choi!

Beggar Consequently, you hate Jesus, don't you?

Leper *(hesitating a while, he answers)* Me hating Jesus? Oh, no! Why should I? How can I possibly hate Jesus himself? *(pause)* Nevertheless... As all the Christians are as stinking as that damned doctor, what's the meaning of me going to church? No use at all. They established a village for lepers, but it's actually a prison, a cage surrounded by invisible high walls. I left it, and wander in the streets as you see me. Even if I go hungry at nearly every mealtime this life is more comfortable for me. *(pause)* If there was, at least, one man like Jesus himself, I might not have been driven out to the streets. Damn the world!

Beggar Now I see a truly foolish fool of you. Better not believe in this Jesus, then, like me! If the church is so crowded just by that kind of Christians, in other word, false and cheating rascals, I'll mostly welcome it being burnt down. I could warm, at least, my frozen body by its burning

거지 그래서 넌 예수를 미워하냐?

문둥이 (잠시 망설이다가) 예수를 미워한다? 천만에! 진짜 예수를 내가 어떻게 미워할 수가 있겠어? (사이) 그렇지만… 예수쟁이들이 온통 저 꼴이니 성당엔 나가서 뭘 해? 무슨 소용이 있겠어? 문둥이촌이라고 만들어 논 건 창살 없는 감옥이고… 그래서 이렇게 떠돌아다니는 거야. 이렇게 사는 게 더 편해. 밥 먹듯이 굶기는 해도 말야. (사이) 진짜 예수가 이 세상에 한 사람만 있어도 내 신세가 이렇진 않을 거야. 에이 빌어먹을!

거지 넌 정말 병신이구나? 아예 나처럼 믿지나 말지. 그 따위 엉터리 사기꾼 같은 쟁이들만 우글거리는 교회라면 불이나 나라지. 추운데 불이나 쬐게….

fire. What else can its building be useful for?

LEPER Useless to speak more about these dirty sons of a bitch. They preach the poor are blessed, but, in reality, the wealthy people get together only among themselves. Oh, this murdering cold!

BEGGAR Yeah, this is seriously killing us.

LEPER Shall we jump?

BEGGAR O.K. Let's jump up to the sky. Now, you start the aria of beggars!

LEPER O.K. You just follw me!

Both of them sing in a sad comic tone the aria of beggars:

If you say one buck,
I should say one duck,
because I like the flesh of the duck
which knows nothing of a buck...

In a moment they dance to the song.

BEGGAR *(abruptly stops his song and dance)* Hey, here comes a duck.

문둥이　더러운 자식들이지. 가난한 자에게 복이 있다고 떠들면서도 사실은 부자들끼리만 서로 싸고 돌거든. 어 추워.

거지　정말 더럽게 춥다.

문둥이　뛸까?

거지　뛰자. 읊어라.

문둥이　그래, 읊자.

문둥이와 거지가 각설이 타령을 부르며 춤을 춘다.

일자 한자 들고보니
일편단심 먹은 마음
죽으면 죽었지 못 잊겠다…

거지　(갑자기 노래와 동작을 멈추고) 야, 하나 온다.

Leper *(also quickly stops)* Where is your duck?

Beggar *(indicating with his finger to the right of the stage)* There! A woman. Maybe a jackpot this time. Let's be prepared quickly for our business.

Both of them prostrate behind their cans. An old woman, actually a pimp, enters from the right wearing a gorgeous head scarf that does not so well suit her age.

Old Woman *(looks around)* Last evening I caught a big fish right here. *(looks at her wristwatch. Pause)* It seems a little early now. Just a little later, young bellies will start feeling itchy. *(clears her throat)* Hum, hum... I'd better exercise my voice till then. *(pause. In a seducing tone)* They are waiting for you, sir. Of course, terribly beautiful girls. All fresh virgins who have never ever had any contact with a man. *(aside)* How about contact among themselves? Why should I know that? *(in a seducing tone again)* You just choose your own taste. What did you say? Money? Oh, I'd say enjoy first and pay later! Who the hell of idiot will do pay first and enjoy later? *(winks*

문둥이 (노래를 같이 멈추고) 어디?

거지 (무대 오른쪽을 가리키며) 저기! 아줌마다. 이번엔 땡이로구나! 빨리 판 벌이자.

문둥이와 거지가 깡통 뒤에 엎드린다. 오른쪽에서 나이에 어울리지 않게 화려한 머리수건을 쓴 아주머니가 걸어 들어온다.

아주머니 (사방을 휘휘 둘러보며) 어젠 여기서 큰 고기를 낚았지. (시계를 본다. 사이) 시간이 좀 이르긴 해. 젊은 놈들 아랫배에 바람 들어갈 시간은 아냐. (목청을 가다듬는다) 흐흠, 그럼 연습을 해 볼까? (사이)
멋진 아가씨 있어요. 딱지도 떼지 않은 숫처녀죠. (혼잣말로) 숫처녀 좋아하네. 내가 알게 뭐야? (다시 유혹하는 어조로) 손님, 자, 이리로. 넷? 돈이요? 아, 기분 내고 돈 내지, 누가 돈 내고 기분 낸답니까? (보이지 않는 손님에게 눈짓하며) 자, 자, 살결이 보송보송한 처녀, 사

to an invisible customer) Now, look! Just believe me, sir. A virgin girl with the most tender skin you will meet. A virgin girl more fresh than an apple, too. I gathered a lot of girls of various style. No doubt you can find a kind exactly suitable to your taste! *(in a flattering gesture)* Sir!

Beggar *(like whispering to the leper)* She looks like trading girls over.

Leper *(in a low voice)* An old bitch of the brothel.

Beggar I don't mind begging even this kind. Who knows? Such a bitch might rather throw me a buck.

Leper I'll just put my face on the ground. That kind of a used car spoils my fortune.

Beggar *(loudly)* Oh, merciful, beautiful, plentiful angel! This is just a wretched poor man! Give me a buck, please.

Old Woman *(surprised almost to death)* Good Lord, what a scare!

Beggar *(slyly)* Hee, hee, hee! Don't be surprised and busy like locusts being roasted in a frypan or panicked fleas jumping in an underwear. Please, lady!

과보다 더 싱싱한 처녀, 손님 맘에 딱 드는 처녀가 얼마든지 있죠. (애교를 떨며) 손님…

거지 (문둥이에게 속삭이듯) 처녀장산가 봐.

문둥이 (낮은 목소리로) 사창굴의 마귀할멈이야.

거지 그래도 한번 해 봐야지. 또 알아? 저런 년들이 한푼 던져 줄지 말야.

문둥이 난 그저 엎드려만 있을란다. 저런 중고차는 재수 없거든.

거지 (큰 소리로) 에에, 불쌍한 놈입니다. 한푼 줍쇼.

아주머니 (깜짝 놀라며) 에구머니나!

거지 (능글맞게) 헤헤헤, 뜨거운 냄비 속에서 메뚜기 볶아대듯, 내복 속에서 놀란 벼룩이 톡톡 튀듯 그렇게 놀라진 마십쇼, 아주머니.

OLD WOMAN *(looking disgusted)* Lady you said? Humph!

BEGGAR Oh, lady more beautiful, elegant, gracious than any fresh virgin, please have pity on my most wretched life and throw a buck to me. I hate my life, but can't live without it.

OLD WOMAN *(in a quick tone)* What the devil's this? You'd better be frozen to death while begging! How dare you make fun of me! *(putting on airs in a scolding tone)* You rat! You never see your long life, if you make a mock of an old lady like this. Spit-spit! Good God! My good luck is now soured!

BEGGAR *(unabashed)* Make a mock of you? God forbid me! I didn't even imagine that. Speaking as frankly as a man showing his two balls under the loin, I'm counted less than a creeping earthworm. I don't have even a drop of energy now to mock the others. I say the truth, nothing but the truth. My body floats only in the cold and hunger. My life always so poor... *(in a singing tone)* Oh, no, no, no, don't talk me off! Now, look, I'm entering. I'm entering. Very well and deeply entering. You, too, entering,

아주머니 (기분이 잡친 듯) 아주머니?

거지 숫처녀보다 더 멋지고 품위 있고 우아하신 아주머니, 이 모진 목숨 불쌍히 보시고 한푼만 톡 던져 줍쇼.

아주머니 (빠른 어조로) 아니, 이런 배라먹다 얼어 뒈질 거지새끼가 날 놀려? (점잖을 빼며 준엄한 목소리로) 이놈! 나이 든 부인네를 희롱하면 오래 못 살아. 에이, 재수에 옴 붙었다. (땅에 침을 뱉으며) 퉤!

거지 (천연덕스럽게) 놀리다뇨? 정말 불알 두 쪽을 톡 까놓고 말이지, 우리 같은 무지렁이가 어디 남을 놀리고 말고 할 기운이나 있습니까요? 춥고 배고픈 인생, 가련한 목숨…
에헤야 에헤, 자, 씨구씨구 들어간다. 잘도 잘도 들어간다. 너도 나도 들어간다.

me, too, entering, everybody entering. Very well and deeply!

Leper If you wish to enjoy long life, if you desire to receive small blessings and big ones as well, please, show some mercy on us the most poor and pitiful.

Old Woman *(jumps up in surprise)* Good heavens! Another devil! *(covering her nose with both hands)* Ouch! What a smell!

Beggar If you give me a buck you'll be blessed by ten bucks. Hee, hee, hee! Show mercy!

Old Woman I never care of your blessing. Ouch! This stinking smell! Because of this stench, smelling as if the whole world were decaying and collapsing, my good luck, this evening, is cursed.

Beggar My gracious lady, a legion of starved devils cry in my empty belly now.

Leper My jawbones, upper and lower, dance hitting each other, and my teeth shake such...wild... ly...la...dy...oh...

The old woman, angry to the top of her head, tries to wave her fist wildly, but stops. She thinks for a while, then,

문둥이 오래오래 사시려면, 큰 복 작은 복 다 받으시려면 불쌍한 놈 동정해 줍쇼.

아주머니 (펄쩍 뛰며) 이건 또 뭐야 (코를 쥐며) 히유우, 이 냄새!

거지 한푼 주면 열푼 버는 복이 굴러 옵죠. 에헤에헤, 적선합쇼.

아주머니 복이고 나발이고, 아휴, 이 냄새! 온 세상이 썩어 무너지는 이 지독한 냄새 때문에 오늘 재수에 옴 붙었다!

거지 뱃가죽이 땡깁니다요, 아주머니!

문둥이 아래 위 턱이 춤추고, 이빨들이 덜덜덜… 아…주…머…니….

taking out a buck from her purse, crumples and throws it to the beggar.

Old Woman Get lost out of here quickly, if you are afraid to be a frozen fish! *(aside)* They have spoiled my business today.

As she hurriedly goes out to the left, she and the Sister cross each other on the way.

Beggar *(grabbing the currency note)* I told you! Rather that kind of a bitch is more helpful to me.

Leper Jackpot! Let's get lost as she demanded. Too cold now to endure anymore.

Beggar We the poor can be wealthy only in patience. There comes a virgin woman in black dress.

Leper Really?

Beggar *(indicating to the left with his chin)* Look to the left!

Leper Aha! An angel. No, not that, but just a shadow of an angel. She's a doll. A doll that has no eyes, no ears, no breast, therefore, no heart.

Beggar You missed the mark. Always! She's a virgin!

아주머니 (화가 머리끝까지 뻗쳐 주먹을 휘두르려다가 멈추고, 잠시 생각해본 뒤 허리춤에서 지폐를 한 장 꺼내 구겨서 거지에게 던진다) 동태되기 전에 여기서 썩 꺼져! (혼잣말로) 오늘 장산 잡쳤다.

아주머니가 왼쪽으로 급히 나갈 때 마주 오는 수녀와 엇갈린다.

거지 (지폐를 움켜쥐면서) 거봐. 저런 년이 오히려 적선한다구.

문둥이 땡잡았다. 가자. 추워서 못 견디겠다.

거지 가만있어. 저기 까만 옷 입은 처녀가 온다.

문둥이 어디?

거지 (턱으로 왼쪽을 가리키며) 저기.

문둥이 아하, 천사다! 아니다, 천사 껍데기다. 인형, 눈도 귀도 가슴도 없는 인형이다.

거지 아니다, 처녀다.

The Sister, sunken in her own deep thinking, murmurs something to herself. She enters from the left.

Beggar Oh, no, no, no... I'm entering. Please show me your mercy of a buck.

Leper We are the most poor and pitiful!

Pretending not to hear their voices, she goes out to the right.

Beggar We got a suicide goal.

Leper That, too, is a Christian, of course, false. I've knowledge on that kind of woman. The outside of them is wrapped quite nice and beautiful, but their inside is full of white bones. They move around busily showing up, as if doing all the good things by themselves alone. But, when nobody is looking at them, they don't lift even a finger. I have, you know, enough knowledge about that kind.

Beggar Her inside seems really full of white bones, as you told me. Then, why are there so many false ones, beyond our count, among these people

수녀가 깊은 생각에 잠겨 혼잣말로 중얼거리면서 왼쪽으로 걸어 나온다.

거지 에에, 씨구씨구, 한푼 줍쇼.

문둥이 불쌍한 놈입니다.

수녀는 못 들은 척하고 그대로 지나쳐 오른쪽으로 나간다.

거지 날샜다.

문둥이 저것도 가짜 예수쟁이야. 저런 건 내가 좀 알지. 껍데기만 그럴듯하게 포장했지만 속은 가짜거든. 좋은 일은 도맡아 하는 것처럼 싸돌아다니지만 남이 안 보는 데선 손가락 하나 까닥 안 해. 저런 건 내가 알아.

거지 가짜긴 정말 가짠 모양이군. 근데 예수쟁이란 놈들은 왜 그렇게 가짜가 많아?

called Christians?

Leper Cause they suffer from indigestion after drinking the water of truth. They desire the water, but can't keep it in their soul. *(The beggar shows a smile of disbelief.)* Damn it! All of them are false. No exception...

Beggar If we don't believe this Jesus, then, we can be the men of truth, not of falsity. Ouch! There comes another woman. This time we might see a true one.

A prostitute enters from the right.

Leper I know that bitch. She entertains in a bar... A dirty prostitute...

Beggar A prostitute or not, I don't mind. Who knows such a wretched woman might be better than a false Christian?

Prostitute *(Stops and, taking out a rouge from her handbag, paints her lips red. Aside)* My God! My skin had never met such a terrible cold. Everything in the world, except beds, seems frozen.

Beggar I'll pray to the God of the Great Bear for you.

문둥이 진짜 물을 먹긴 먹었는데 소화불량에 걸렸거든. (거지가 피식 웃는다) 모조리 가짜야, 쳇!

거지 예수를 안 믿으면 진짜 사람이 되겠다. 이크! 또 하나 온다. 저건 진짤지도 모르겠다.

오른쪽으로 창녀가 걸어 들어온다.

문둥이 저 년은 내가 알아. 술집에 다녀. 갈보년이야.

거지 갈보면 어때? 가짜 예수쟁이보다 더 좋을지 누가 알어?

창녀 (걸음을 멈추고 손가방에서 립스틱을 꺼내 입술을 다시 칠하면서 혼잣말로) 원, 지겹게도 춥네. 침대만 빼고 모조리 얼어버리겠어.

Then, very soon, you can meet your most wonderful lover. Oh, no, no, no, don't tell me no. Give me a buck, young lady.

Leper I'm so hungry.

Prostitute *(mimicking the beggar)* Give me a buck, young lady? Pew! *(puts her rouge back in her handbag)* Don't make me laugh! You are spoiling my good luck.

Beggar This body of mine can neither make the others laugh, nor laugh by itself. I'm just a wanderer. The day I am luckily given a cup of wine, free of charge, it is always as good as my birthday. The whole world has no equals with us in our pitiful life.

Prostitute Why should you talk so much?

Beggar Even if I have no money in my pockets, I can be wealthy, at least, in my talking. Why shouldn't I? The young lady's now waiting for her good husband, isn't she?

Prostitute *(in a self-contemptuous tone)* Good husband? You crazy! That kind of animal, I mean good husband, is now an item to be exhibited in a museum. Not a bit interesting to me.

거지 가시는 길에 좋은 님 만나도록 칠성님께 빌어 드리죠. 에헤야디이야. 한푼만 적선합쇼, 아기씨.

문둥이 배가 고파요.

창녀 적선? 흥! (립스틱을 손가방에 집어넣고) 웃기지 말어. 재수 없게.

거지 웃기지도 못하고 웃지도 못하는 인생. 술이라도 한잔 얻어 걸리는 날이 생일 잔칫날인 떠돌이 인생. 가련하기로는 이 세상에 그 짝이 없는 놈들입네다.

창녀 웬 말이 이렇게 많아?

거지 돈이 없으면 말이라도 많아얍죠. 아가씬 지금 낭군을 기다리는 모양이죠?

창녀 (자조적인 어조로) 낭군? 흥! 낭군 좋아하네. 그 따윈 박물관에나 진열하는 거야. 난 흥미 없어.

Beggar In a museum or out I don't care. Anyway give me a buck.

Prostitute *(inclining her head to a side, aside)* Shall I give him a buck? Who knows my fortune of today may be doubled by this good gesture? *(taking out a currency note out of her handbag, she throws it to the beggar.)*

Beggar Wow! Millions of thanks to you! The God of the Great Bear grant you a mountain of blessing! *(creeps to take the money)*

Prostitute Blessing of the God of the Great Bear? Even that, the more, the better. *(aside)* I'm sure I'll be so lucky today. I'd welcome any guy, even an old monster, if he pays a plenty. Humph! A plenty of money.... *(chewing peppermint gum noisily, she goes out to the left)*

Beggar Look at this! Isn't a prostitute a hundred times better than a Christian? What do you say?

Leper I've nothing to say.

Beggar *(shrieking joyously, he stands on his hands.)* A prostitute is a thousand times more merciful than a Christian! *(pause)*

Leper *(all of a sudden)* Shhht! The monster! He comes here.

거지 그건 그거고, 동정합쇼.

창녀 (고개를 갸우뚱거리며 혼잣말로) 한 장 던질까? 재수가 곱 기로 굴러 떨어질지 누가 알겠어? (손가방에서 백 원짜리 지폐 한 장을 꺼내 거지에게 던진다)

거지 아이구, 고마우셔라. 칠성님은 삼태기로 복을 내려 주소서! (기어가서 돈을 집는다)

창녀 칠성님의 복? 그거라도 많으면 좋지. (혼잣말로) 오늘은 재수가 있을 거야. 늙은이라도 돈이나 많이 주는 자식이 걸려라. 흥! 돈이라… (껌을 요란하게 씹으면서 왼쪽으로 나간다)

거지 이것 봐. 갈보년이 예수쟁이보다 백 배 낫지? 어때?

문둥이 난 할 말 없다.

거지 (기성을 지르며 물구나무서기를 한다) 갈보년이 예수쟁이보다 천배는 자비롭다! (사이)

문둥이 (갑자기) 쉬이잇! 떴다, 떴어.

The beggar stops as quickly as a flash standing on his hands. Putting the money in his pocket, he prostrates on the ground. The leper also prostrates, frozen still. Pause. A policeman comes out from the right, a baton in his hand. He approaches with very arrogant steps.

POLICEMAN *(mockingly, he inspects them from various angles. At last, he kicks the beggar.)* You rascal! What are you doing here? Stand up! *(The beggar does not move an inch, as if dead. The policeman kicks more violently.)* You son of a bitch! Are you deaf? Already a dead body are you? I told you to stand up!

BEGGAR *(reluctantly raising his head)* Please overlook my fault, sir.

POLICEMAN What are you doing here?

BEGGAR As you see me...

POLICEMAN If anyone makes, without a cause, a passerby feel unpleasant, he violates the Law of Punishing Light Crimes. You know that very well, don't you? Who did permit you to beg here as you like? Now, go back to your home quickly. I say... quickly!

BEGGAR I've no home, sir.

거지가 잽싸게 물구나무서기를 그만두고 돈을 주머니에 넣은 뒤 엎드린다. 문둥이도 엎드린 채 꼼짝도 않는다. 사이. 오른쪽에서 한 손에 방망이를 든 경찰이 걸어 나온다. 매우 거만한 걸음걸이다.

경찰 (놀리듯 거지와 문둥이를 이러 저리 훑어보다가 거지를 발로 툭 차면서) 야, 여기서 뭘 하고 있어? 일어나! (거지가 죽은 듯이 꼼짝도 안하자 조금 세게 걷어찬다) 이 새끼, 안 들려? 벌써 송장이야? 일어나!

거지 (마지못해 고개를 든다) 나리, 봐 줍쇼.

경찰 뭐 하고 있어?

거지 보시는 바와 같이…

경찰 지나가는 사람들을 공연히 불쾌하게 만들면 경범죄 처벌법에 걸린다는 걸 몰라? 누가 멋대로 구걸하라고 했어? 자, 빨랑빨랑 집으로 꺼져!

거지 집이 없는뎁쇼?

Policeman It's your business, not mine. Anyway, get out of here! *(thrusts his baton on the leper's body here and there)* What's this? Another rascal here, too. You stand up! You dirty cursed beggars destroy the tourist industry of our country. Aren't you ashamed of that?

Leper *(raises his head)* Just once, please, overlook me, sir.

Policeman If you freeze to death here, the troublesome work to clear your body comes only to me. I'm in charge of this street, you know. You dare disobey my order? Get away! Now!

Beggar I'll do my greatest best not to be frozen dead, sir. Therefore, don't worry anything, nothing, sir.

Leper *(shaking his body violently)* Oh, Jesus! Jesus! Jesus! *(crosses himself)*

Policeman *(looking dubious)* Jesus? What kind of Jesus? Do you think Jesus is the owner of a blanket producing company? In this sharp cold, why do you come and sit here?

Leper You aren't a Christian, are you? Sir?

Policeman I'm not interested in the childish story. Are you one of them?

Leper I had been, once.

경찰 내가 알게 뭐야? 하여간 꺼져! (방망이로 문둥이를 쿡쿡 쑤시며) 이건 또 뭐야? 야, 일어나! 니들 거지새끼들 때문에 관광사업이 안 된다구.

문둥이 (고개를 들고) 한 번만 봐 줍쇼.

경찰 여기서 얼어 뒈지면 나만 귀찮아져. 여긴 내 관할구역이란 말야. 꺼지지 못해?

거지 얼어 죽지 않도록 최대한 노력할 테니 염려 팍 놓으십쇼, 나리.

문둥이 (덜덜 떨면서) 예수! 예수! 예수! (가슴에 성호를 긋는다)

경찰 (의아해하며) 뭐, 예수? 예수가 담요공장 사장인 줄 알아? 추운데 왜 여기 나와 앉아 있는거냐?

문둥이 나리는 예수쟁이 아니시죠?

경찰 그 따위 얘긴 흥미 없어. 넌 쟁이냐?

문둥이 한땐 그랬죠.

Policeman *(raising up the leper's chin with the baton)* Then, did that Jesus teach you to live by begging here?

Beggar Do us a favour, sir. Just pretend not to see us, sir.

Leper We expect nothing else from you, sir. You don't need to give us a buck, sir.

Policeman *(looking bored)* Ah, these hopeless rascals! I'd better overlook. Frozen dead or not, it's your own business. I've nothing to do with it. Do you understand? Oh, what the hell this cold is! *(folds his arms and goes out to the right)*

Beggar *(whispering)* I...I... at last shook off the devil from my neck.

Leper Though a young chicken, that monster is quite gentle. He knows even how to overlook something. So quick in his learning!

Beggar Damn it! Too cold to think anything.

Leper Let's dance.

Beggar Why not?

They stand up and start a dance of the crippled people. They sing a song of beggars, too. Lights fade out slowly.

경찰 (방망이로 문둥이 턱을 받치며) 그 예수가 너더러 여기서 빌어먹으라고 가르쳤냐?

거지 (사정하듯) 제발 못 본 척만 해 주십쇼, 나리.

문둥이 동냥은 안 주셔도 좋습니다, 나리.

경찰 (귀찮은 듯이) 에이, 오라질 놈들! 봐 줬다. 얼어 뒈지든지 맘대로 해. 난 모르겠다. 어 추워. (팔짱을 끼고 오른쪽으로 나간다)

거지 (속삭이듯) 하…학질 뗐다.

문둥이 젊은 놈이 제법이다. 봐 줄 줄도 알고.

거지 에이 추워. 염병할.

문둥이 읊자.

거지 그래.

거지와 문둥이가 일어서서 병신춤을 추면서 씨구씨구 타령을 하는 동안 조명이 천천히 나간다.

Act Three

front ground of the church

A small part of a Catholic church is seen on the right side of the stage and the left of the church is its front ground. A bronze statue of Jesus, actually an actor, is standing at the left corner of the ground. Jesus wears a gilded crown with a bronze stick at hand. The Sister prays in front of the statue. After a while, she stands up and goes out to the left. Pause. Drinking from a bottle of local wine, the leper staggers out from the right.

LEPER *(already quite drunken)* Wine! Wine is my best friend! When crushed by a heavy burden of agony, we can't be consoled by anything in the world. But, wine! The only consolation of mine! My flesh goes rotting deeper and deeper,

제3장

성당 마당

성당 건물이 오른쪽에 조금 보이고 왼쪽으로 마당이다. 무대 왼쪽 구석에 청동 예수상이 서 있다. 예수는 도금한 관을 쓰고 청동 지팡이를 짚고 있다. 동상 앞에 수녀가 무릎을 꿇은 채 잠시 기도를 바치다가 일어서서 왼쪽으로 나간다. 사이. 문둥이가 술병을 입에 댄 채 오른쪽에서 비틀거리며 나온다.

문둥이 (혀가 꼬부라져서) 술, 술이 제일이다. 마음이 괴로운 놈에겐 무조건 술이다. 살이 썩어 들어가다 보면 죽기밖에 더하겠어? 어차피 죽을 목숨인데… 음…

someday I'll be no more in this world, but why should I worry about that? Everybody would die. Nobody can live in this world forever. Some day or the other... Matter of time... Hum... *(staggering)* Crushed by agony? This cursed body is more suffering than the mind. Yeah, my body... Pain? I don't care nothing. Wine keeps me going *(drinks)*
Hey, you beggar! I don't know even your name, but anyway thank you. In this large, immense world, nobody but you gave me a drink. How kind! Thank you so much! *(pause)*
Eh? What's this? This is an ear, oh, my ear! *(bowing low, he picks up his fallen ear and puts it in his pocket)* Now one of my ears dropped on the ground, then, tomorrow my nose'll disappear. Hello, you leper! How wonderful a shape you show! Serve you right! Just a moment ago the girl said. The girl, like a used car, said I'd better die quickly. Well, if I did as she said, somebody might have brought my dead body to a crematorium.
(Before he knows it, his body hits the statue's pedestal.

(비틀거리며) 마음이 괴롭다구? 몸이 더 괴롭지, 몸이! 아냐, 괴로울 것도 없다. 술이 있으니까 괜찮아. (마신다)
거지야, 이름도 모르는 거지야, 고맙다. 이렇게 술 사주는 놈은 이 세상에 너 하나뿐이로구나. (사이)
어라? 귀가! 내 귀가! (허리를 굽혀 땅에 떨어진 자기 귀를 집어 주머니에 넣는다) 귀가 떨어졌으니 내일은 코가 없어지겠지. 이 문둥아! 꼴좋다, 좋아. 아까 중고차 같은 여자 말대로 칵 뒈져 버리기라도 했다면 화장터에서나 데려가지.
(무심코 동상 받침대에 부딪쳐 놀란 시선으로 동상을 쳐다본다) 이건 뭐야? 예수? (동상을 만져보다가 눈이 둥그래진다) 히야, 이거 순 구리로구나! (사이) 값이 꽤 나가겠는 걸? 가만 있자. 한 근에 오백 원 잡고… 이게 몇 근이나 될까… 한 오백 근 나갈까? 그러면 오백 원에다가 오백 근이면… 이거 산수마저 다 까먹었으

He looks up at the statue with surprised eyes) What the hell is this? Eh? Jesus? *(touching the bronze statue, he is so much surprised again)* Wow! This is pure, pure bronze! *(pause)* Maybe very expensive, isn't it? No hurry, calm down and count... 5 dollars a pound... How much weight? Around 500 pounds? Then, 500 times 5 dollars makes... My God! I forgot how to count... No matter. This will bring a great money. Sure.
If I take this and sell, I can eat for a long while plenty of white bread and meat soup. My stomach may burst of too much food. No, not the food first. I've to buy an overcoat first of all. *(shivering)* Oh, what a cold! Yes, I'll buy underwears and a wool sweater, shoes and a neckerchief... Hee, hee, hee! I can get anything! Well, before buying a thing... I should have first my disease cured. When the flesh and bones decay in the body, what's the use of fine outwears? It's like a golden apple with its inside totally rotten!
Now, this lump of bronze... *(pause)* Jesus... bronze... Jesus... bronze... Jesus... bronze...

니… 좌우지간 엄청나겠다.
이걸 갖다 팔면 흰 쌀밥에 고깃국을 배 터지게 먹겠다. 아니, 우선 잠바를 하나 사야지. (몸을 떨며) 어 추워. 그래, 내복도 쉐타도 구두도 목도리도… 야, 뭐든지 다 살 수 있겠다. 그것보다도… 병부터 고쳐야지. 안에서 살과 뼈가 썩고 있는데 좋은 옷 걸쳐서 무슨 소용이야? 빛 좋은 개살구지.
그래, 이놈의 구리 덩어리를… (사이) 예수… 구리… 예수… 구리… 예수… 구리… 구리, 구리, 돈! (동상을 손톱으로 긁으며) 아이구, 내 손톱이야! (사이)
그런데 이걸 어떻게 뜯어 간다? 칼로 긁어? 톱으로 잘라내? 도끼로 부셔? 잠깐! 잠깐! 이걸 들고 가다가 경찰한테 잡혀? 아이구, 맙소사! 그렇지만 이건 순 돈덩어린데… 어떡한다? (사이)
아냐, 이건 나쁜 생각이다. 도둑질이야. 그것도 예수를… (사이. 반발하며) 이건 예수가 아

bronze... and money! *(scratching the statue with his fingernails)* Ouch! My fingernails broken! *(pause)* How can I take this away, then?
How to break? Cut by knife? Slice by a thaw? Break by an axe? Wait! Wait a moment! While I pull this away, I may be arrested by a policeman. The devilish policeman! How terrible guy! Zeus help me! But, this is a nice chance for my great money... What shall I do?
(after a pause, rethinking) I was thinking in a wicked way. No, I shouldn't do anything with this. How can I steal, and that stealing Jesus? *(Pause, reacting angrily)* Jesus? No, this is not Jesus. This is a fake. Simply a huge lump of bronze. Damned all the sons of a bitch! What kind of sons of a bitch made such a lifeless thing and collected money from empty heads? They never gave a coin to me, a leper. *(pause)*
Not even a sheet of blanket with me, how can I go through this cold night? Where I sleep? No idea. Well, que sera sera, what will be will be! Now I've nothing to do but drink. *(drinks again. To the statue)*

냐. 가짜야. 단순한 구리 덩어리야. 망할 놈들 같으니! 어떤 자식이 이따위 걸 만들자고 돈을 거뒀어? 문둥이에게 단 한푼도 동냥하지 않는 놈들이! (사이)

담요 한 장 없으니 오늘밤은 어떻게 한다? 어디서 자? 에라, 모르겠다. 술이나 마시자. (다시 술을 마신다)

야, 허수아비 예수! 한잔 할래? 쳇! 구리 덩어리가 술은 무슨 술? 피도 눈물도 심장도 입도 없는 구리 예수! 이 가짜야! (발길로 동상 받침대를 마구차고 주먹으로 동상을 때린다) 진짜 예수는 너처럼 구경만 하진 않아. 부자들에게만 귀여움 받는 장난감이 아니란 말이다.

Hey, you Jesus, you scarecrow! You want a drink, eh? Pshaw! How can a lump of bronze drink? Impossible fantasy! Bronze Jesus, you have no blood, no tears, no heart, no mouth. You are a fake! *(kicks and slaps the statue's pedestal violently)* The real, true Jesus doesn't just look around like you. He isn't a toy, I mean, a favourite of the wealthy people only.

JESUS *(faint smile on his lips)* You are right.

LEPER *(surprised to death)* Dear me! A ghost! A devil! Oh, a statue speaks! *(pause)* Am I crazy?

JESUS Don't be surprised. I am Jesus.

LEPER *(more surprised)* Wha... What did you say? Damned me! Am I dreaming now? Let me see it. *(pricks his cheeks)* What's the use of pricking my cheeks? Am I not a leper? Anyway, it's true I'm not dreaming. Now I know! That's the devil. Sure the devil has come to catch me. The devil in the guise of Jesus. Oh, I'm terrified to death! The devil is hidden behind the statue! *(retreating, tries to run away)*

JESUS Don't be afraid of me! I just wish to talk with you. I have been waiting truly so long time

예수 (은근히 미소를 머금으며) 당신 말이 맞소.

문둥이 (소스라치게 놀라며) 으악! 도깨비다! 귀신이다! 동상이 말을 하다니! (사이) 내가 미쳤는가?

예수 놀라지 마시오. 난 예수요.

문둥이 (더욱 놀라며) 뭐…뭐라구? 내가 꿈을 꾸고 있나? 어디 보자. (자기 볼을 꼬집어본다) 문둥인데 꼬집어 봐선 뭘 해? 그렇지만 꿈이 아닌 건 분명해. 그래, 저건 악마다. 틀림없이 악마가 날 잡으려고 온 거야. 예수의 탈을 쓴 악마. 아, 무서워. 악마가 저 뒤에 숨어 있는 거야. (뒷걸음질 치며 달아나려고 한다)

예수 두려워하지 마시오. 난 당신과 이야기하고 싶소. 참으로 긴 세월을 기다려 왔소. 나하고 대화 나눌 사람을… 병들고 헐벗고 굶주리고 천대받는 사람들이 모두 나의 형제요 자매입니다. 그런데 나를 믿는다고 자처하는 자들, 나를 따르는 제자라고 자랑하는 자들이 나의 형제를 무시하고 억압하고 있소. 나는 당신이

to find a man to talk to. The sick, the naked, the hungry, the mistreated, all of them are my brothers and my sisters. But, those who call themselves Christians, those who boast of their being my disciples, they are disdaining and oppressing my brothers. I know very well the reality that you suffer leprosy and your body always shivers in front of the threatening cold and hunger. I wish to help you. But, you have to help me first.

LEPER *(deriding)* Ha, ha, ha, ha! Did you say I'm your brother? You are my elder brother, I'm your younger brother? Pshaw! Do you think you can cheat me by such words sweet only to the ears? None of your tricks with me! Never! Hey, you fake Jesus! Don't you know these false Christians, too. preach just like you everyday, and everywhere? How easy the preaching is to them! *(spits on the ground)* Spit-spit! How disgusting! My fortune of tomorrow is cursed!

JESUS *(aside)* Alas! Because of those who serve me only by their lips, because of those wicked hypocrites, even good souls are afflicted so

문둥병에 시달리고, 추위와 기아의 위협 앞에 항상 떨고 있는 현실을 잘 알고 있습니다. 당신을 도와주고 싶습니다. 그러나 당신이 먼저 날 도와주어야겠소.

문둥이 (조소하며) 하하하하. 내가 너의 형제라고? 네가 형님, 내가 동생? 흥! 그 따위 귀에 달콤한 소리로 날 꾀어넘기려고 해? 어림 반 푼어치도 없지, 없어! 이 가짜 예수야! 예수쟁이들도 그런 소린 식은 죽 먹기로 하고 다녀. (땅에 침을 뱉으며) 퉤! 나 더러워서… 내일 재수에 옴 붙었다.

예수 (혼잣말로) 아아, 슬프구나. 입으로만 나를 섬기는 무리, 사악한 위선자들 때문에 착한 영혼까지 저렇게 심한 불신의 병에 걸려 있다니! 말로는 버림받은 영혼을 동정한다면서 손으로는 그들의 속옷까지 가로채 가는 자들, 진실을 버린 자들… 껍데기 신자가 너무 득시글거리는 세상이구나…. 아아, 진실한 제자를 단 한명이라도 이 땅에서 만나보고 싶구나! (사

gravely by the disease of disbelief! With their lips, these false Christians confess their pitying the abandoned souls, but, with their hands, they snatch away even the poor's underwears. They really discard the truth, my truth... The world is full of too many fake Christians, I realise now. Ah, I wish to meet my true disciples, even one true disciple on the ground! *(Pause. To the leper)* Now, come nearer to me.

LEPER *(more alarmed)* You... you try to drag me away? No, never! You are the devil disguised by the mask of Jesus, I know! How dare you cheat me unto your snare.

JESUS Just moment ago you said you wished to take this lump of bronze, didn't you?

LEPER *(surprised again)* Damn me! How... how this... I'm not a thief. I never steal anything. You cursed devil!

JESUS This shining gilded bronze crown, bronze stick, bronze clothes, bronze shoes, all these you may take away. Yes, take them away now. Sell them in the market, and fill your empty stomach with as much food as you want.

이. 문둥이에게) 자, 이리로 가까이 오십시오.

문둥이 (더욱 경계하면서) 날, 날 잡아가려구? 안 돼, 이 예수 탈을 쓴 악마야! 누가 속을 줄 알아?

예수 조금 전에 이 구리를 가져가고 싶다고 하지 않았소?

문둥이 (놀라며) 아니, 저게… 난 도…둑질 안 해. 이 빌어먹을 악마새끼야.

예수 번쩍번쩍 금칠한 이 구리관, 구리지팡이, 구리옷, 구리신발 모두 벗겨서 당신이 가져가시오. 시장에 내다 팔아서 배불리 먹으시오. 난 이런 쓸데없는 장식품에 갇혀서 답답해 죽을 지경이오.

Imprisoned in these useless decorative things, I'm nearly suffocated.

Leper *(suspicious and cautious)* Did you say I might take away these...?

Jesus Yes, I said it clearly. Sell out all these, and, first of all, have a hearty meal, put on warm clothes.

Leper *(defiantly)* You cursed rascal! Now you change your trick and try to seduce me by these lumps of bronze. Damn you! Come with your best snare, but I'll never be fooled! Yes, it's impossible forever! I've nothing to do with the devil like you. You have missed your mark greatly.

Jesus *(in a sad tone)* It's no wonder you don't believe me. You fail to recognise me, because I wasn't such Jesus before, My followers who look quite normal outwardly but rotten inwardly put this heavy gold crown on my head, and a bronze stick in my hand. Wrapping my whole body with the bronze clothes, they made it impossible for me to move an inch. Ah, how stifling these are! They threw me in a bronze prison, and now turn their face about even to

문둥이 (의아하고도 조심스러워서) 가져가라구?

예수 그래요, 이걸 몽땅 팔아서 우선 배불리 먹고 따뜻하게 옷을 사 입으시오.

문둥이 (삿대질을 하며) 너 이 자식! 이제는 구리덩어릴 가지고 날 꾀이려는 거지? 피이, 안 속는다, 안 속아. 난 너 같은 악마하고는 절대 인연이 없어. 너 사람 한번 잘못 봤어.

예수 (슬픈 목소리로) 당신이 날 믿지 않는 것도 무리는 아니오. 난 본래 이런 예수가 아니었으니까 당신이 날 몰라보는 거요. 겉은 멀쩡해도 속이 썩은 신자들이 이렇게 내 머리에 무거운 금관을 얹어놓고 손에는 구리막대기, 그리고 온 몸을 구리옷으로 감싸서 날 꼼짝 못하게 만들어 버렸소. 아아, 답답해! 날 구리 감옥에 처넣고 나서 이젠 나의 가르침마저 외면하고 있소. 난 지금 움직일 수가 없소. 가짜 예수쟁이가 내 이름을 팔고, 내 이름을 더럽히고 있는데도 난 저 오만불손한 무리를 이렇게 바라다볼 수밖에 없소. 난 저 무리의 포로요.

my teaching. Until now I couldn't move, still I can't. Even though fake Christians sell out and smear my good name, I can't help myself but just look at this arrogant mob helplessly. I'm now their prisoner, signboard, and commodity. Ah, I can't endure my anxieties anymore.

LEPER *(laughs himself into convulsions)* Ha, ha, ha, ha! A fake curses the other fake! Ha, ha, ha, ha!

JESUS What shall I do for you to make you believe me?

LEPER *(showing some curiosity, but, in a haughty tone)* If you were the true Jesus, you have to reveal your power...hm... why not show me a surprising miracle that's impossible to be done by any man?

JESUS Miracle? Do you want to see a miracle?

LEPER Yeah, I want a miracle.

JESUS *(looks annoyed)* If you don't believe me, seeing me with your own eyes, of what use then is a miracle to you?

LEPER Pshaw! Don't talk nonsense! You can't show me a miracle. You are really a fake. A fake Jesus is more wicked than a false Christian. You are

간판이고 상품이요. 아아, 속이 타서 못 견디겠소.

문둥이 (배를 쥐고 웃으며) 하하하하, 가짜가 가짜를 욕해? 하하하하.

예수 어떻게 하면 날 믿겠소?

문둥이 (호기심이 생겼으나 거만한 어조로) 당신이 진짜 예수라면 말야. 그만한 힘을 보여 주거나… 흠… 사람이 할 수 없는 놀라운 기적을 일으켜 보라구.

예수 기적, 기적을 원한다?

문둥이 그래, 기적…

예수 (안타깝다는 듯이) 눈으로 날 보고도 믿지 않는데 기적 따위가 무슨 소용이란 말이오?

문둥이 쳇! 못하니까 딴 소리야. 넌 가짜가 분명해. 가짜 예수는 가짜 예수쟁이보다 더 악질이야. 넌 가짜야, 악마새끼야. (화를 내며) 너 할 지랄이 없어서, 그래 가짜 예수질을 해? 지옥으로 꺼져! 썩 꺼지지 못해?

a fake. A cursed son of the devil. *(getting angry)* Do you really have nothing to do, so you play the game of fake Jesus? Go to hell! Don't you hear me saying go to hell?

Jesus *(aside)* It's no wonder I'm insulted, because those who boast to be my disciples don't show good examples. Truth, freedom, justice, love, each of these keeps just futile, empty name. While their practical content is trampled in the real life, ah, my disciples, what are they doing? Easy going, idle, and busy to evade their responsibility... Is there not a disciple who really loves me? *(to the leper)* You, my brother! Do you really wish to be liberated from your leprosy?

Leper *(sneering, but, seeming to hope a little)* Why do you talk nonsense? Any leper wishes to be clean, doesn't he?

Jesus Then, come nearer to me. *(Pause. The leper hesitates a while, then moves a step to the statue)* What's that you hold in your hand?

Leper *(raising the bottle)* You mean this? Korean local wine.

예수 (혼잣말로) 나의 제자랍시고 으스대는 자들이 제대로 모범을 보이지 않으니 내가 욕을 먹게도 됐어. 진실도 자유도 정의도 사랑도 모두 허망한 이름만 남았구나! 그 실질적 내용이 현실에서 짓밟히고 있는데, 아아, 나의 제자들은 무엇을 하고 있는가? 안일하고 나태하고 책임 회피에 분주하고… 진실로 날 사랑하는 제자가 한 명도 없는가? (문둥이에게) 당신, 문둥병에서 해방되고 싶소?

문둥이 (냉소하나 약간 희망을 걸 듯) 그런 걸 말이라고 해? 뻔할 뻔자지.

예수 그럼, 이리로 가까이 오시오. (사이. 문둥이가 망설이다가 한걸음 다가간다) 그 손에 든 게 뭐요?

문둥이 (병을 들어 보이며) 이거? 소주.

Jesus Local wine?

Leper *(laughing)* Very strong. It's 30 degrees of alcohol. No side dish I have.

Jesus Will you put some drops into my mouth? If you do that, you can show me you truly love me. Will you? Now, show me your love!

Leper *(very suspicious)* Then... are you... truly Jesus... oh, no... my Lord?

Jesus *(in an authoritative tone)* Now, come nearer.

Leper *(approaching)* Are you really... Jesus Christ... my Lord?

Jesus Do you truly love me?

Leper *(in a shaking voice)* Do I... I love... you? You know my heart better than me. I stopped going to church ten years ago, because I hated to see fakes, but... I never turned my back... to you... *(puts the bottle to the mouth of Jesus, almost weeping)* Drink this wine, please. Sorry I have no side dish to offer.

Jesus *(takes back his lips from the bottle)* Ah, my blood starts to circulate in the vein again. It's been so long! *(to the leper)* Do you believe me?

Leper *(pushing the bottle forward)* Take some more, my

예수 소주?

문둥이 (웃으며) 독한 술이지. 30도, 안주도 없고.

예수 그걸 내 입에 좀 넣어 주겠소? 그래서 당신이 정말 날 사랑한다는 걸 행동으로 보여 주시오.

문둥이 (의심스러운 듯이) 그러면… 네가… 당신… 진짜 예수…님입니까?

예수 (권위 있는 음성으로) 자, 가까이 오시오.

문둥이 (다가가며) 당신이 정말… 예수님이십니까?

예수 당신은 날 사랑하오?

문둥이 (떨리는 목소리로) 그…그것은… 당신이 더 잘 알고 계십니다. 가짜들 꼴이 보기 싫어 10년 동안 성당에 안 나가긴 했지만, 전… 당신을… (예수의 입에다 소주병을 대면 예수가 받아 마신다. 울먹이는 목소리로) 드세요. 안주가 없어서 죄송해요.

예수 (소주병에서 입을 떼며) 아아, 이제야 내 혈관에 피가 다시 도는구나. (문둥이에게) 날 믿소?

문둥이 (병을 내밀며) 더 드세요, 예수님.

Lord.

Jesus You are no more a leper.

Leper *(startled, he drops the bottle)* What?

Jesus Touch your ear.

Leper *(touching his ear)* Oh! My ear came back! *(unfolding, as if crazy, the bandage from his leg)* Oh, it's clean! It's truly clean! *(overjoyed, he dances, jumping. Then, he kneels before Jesus.)* My Lord, pardon me not to have recognised you. *(sobs)*

Jesus *(benevolently)* It's not your fault. It's the sin of those who spread the disease of disbelief all over the world. *(pause)* Now I can't tolerate the defeat of the truth, the silence of the truth any more. You shall be my witness.

Leper If you command, I'll jump even into fire.

Jesus Did you say it with your whole heart?

Leper Yes, my Lord.

Jesus Then, do me a favour.

Leper My Lord requests a favour of me, such a wretched sinner?

예수 당신은 이제 문둥이가 아니오.

문둥이 (소스라치게 놀라 병을 떨어뜨린다) 넷?

예수 당신 귀를 만져 보시오.

문둥이 (자기 귀를 만지며) 앗! 내 귀가! (다리에 감은 붕대를 미친 듯이 풀며) 아아, 정말이다! 정말! (기쁨에 넘쳐 덩실덩실 춤을 추다가 예수 앞에 무릎을 꿇는다) 주여, 몰라 뵌 죄 용서해 주소서. (흐느낀다)

예수 (너그럽게) 그건 당신의 죄가 아니오. 불신의 병을 이 세상에 퍼뜨린 무리의 죄요. (사이) 난 이제 더 이상 진리의 패배, 진실의 침묵을 내버려 둘 수가 없소. 당신은 나의 증인이 되어 주시오.

문둥이 주님께서 시키시는 일이라면 불 속에라도 뛰어들겠습니다.

예수 그 말, 진정이오?

문둥이 네!

예수 그러면 내 부탁을 들어 주시오.

문둥이 저 같은 놈에게 예수님께서 부탁을?

JESUS First, take off from my head this gold crown, no, bronze crown. To me becomes only the thorny crown but the wealthy people disguised me as they liked. Take off my bronze clothes, bronze stick, too. Take away.

LEPER *(waving both hands)* No...no... I can't...

JESUS *(disappointed)* You can't? Even if I ask your favour?

LEPER Even if that... I can't steal. Never!

JESUS You are not stealing. All these I give to you.

LEPER If the others see me... surely it's stealing. My Lord, you can take them off by yourself. can't you?

JESUS If I take them off by myself, it's meaningless, valueless. Only when these are taken off by the help of humble men like you, my salvation works are perfectly fulfilled. Moreover, you need right now the clothes and the food, don't you?

LEPER If you're... stripped of your bronze clothes... Oh, what a cold!

JESUS Now, it's your turn to help me. My false disciples, however numerous, even hundreds

예수 먼저 내 머리에서 이 금관, 아니, 구리관을 벗겨 주시오. 나한텐 가시관이라야 어울리는데 부자들이 제멋대로 날 변장시켰소. 구리옷도 벗겨 가고, 구리 지팡이도 가져가시오.

문둥이 (두 손을 내저으며) 그…그건 안 됩니다.

예수 (실망한 듯) 안 된다? 부탁인데도?

문둥이 아무리 부탁이라도… 전 도둑질은 못합니다. 절대로!

예수 이건 도둑질이 아니오. 내가 주는 것이오.

문둥이 남이 보면 역시… 도둑질이죠. 당신 스스로 벗을 수 있지 않아요, 예수님?

예수 내가 스스로 벗으면 가치가 없소. 당신같이 겸손한 인간의 도움을 받아서 벗어야 구원사업이 이루어지는 거요. 게다다 당신은 지금 당장 옷이 필요하고 밥을 먹어야 하지 않소?

문둥이 그… 구리옷 벗으면… 엇, 추워.

예수 자, 당신이 날 도와줄 차례가 왔소. 가짜 제자들은 수천만이 있어도 날 도와주지 못하지만, 당신만은 날 이 구리 감옥에서 해방시켜줄 수

of millions, can't help me. But there is only one man in the world who can liberate me from this bronze prison. Now!

LEPER I'm a ... nothing like dust. Too exhausted to help you. Furthermore, stripping you bare in this severest cold seems too rude.

JESUS If you don't do me a favour, I should just helplessly look at every kind of injustice, oppression and tragedy which are done on the carth. Watch me! I'm helpless because of this bronze prison. Do you want to keep me helpless forever?

LEPER *(embarrassed)* No... no, I don't. You have to work, my Lord.

JESUS Then, help me. Only when I get rid of this bronze lumps, I can teach the truth and love to the people and make them practise. Of course, I can drive false Christians out of the church, too.

LEPER If it's my Lord's wish... *(makes up his mind)* All right. I'll help you. *(puts forward his shaking hands)* I don't care to be accused of being a thief...for you, my Lord. *(reluctantly strips Jesus of*

있는 거요. 자!

문둥이 전… 보잘 것 없는 놈입니다. 당신을 도와드릴 힘이 없어요. 그리고 이 강추위에 당신을 발가벗긴다는 게 차마…

예수 당신이 도와주지 않는다면 이 땅에서 일어나고 있는 온갖 불의와 억압과 비극을 그냥 바라보고 있을 수밖에 없소. 보시오! 이 구리 감옥 때문이오. 그래도 좋소?

문둥이 (당황해지며) 아…아니… 그건 안 됩니다. 예수님께서 일을 하셔야죠.

예수 그럼 날 도와주시오. 이 구리 덩어리를 벗어나야만 내가 진실과 사랑을 사람들에게 가르치고, 실천하게 만들 수 있소. 가짜 예수쟁이들도 교회에서 몰아내고….

문둥이 주님의 뜻이 정 그러시다면… (결심한 듯) 좋아요. 도와드리죠. (손을 떨면서 내민다) 도둑으로 몰려도 좋아요, 예수님을 위해서라면… (마지못해 하면서 예수의 구리관, 지팡이, 옷, 신발을 벗겨서 땅바닥에 놓는다)

his bronze crown, bronze stick, clothes, and shoes. He puts them down on the ground.)

JESUS *(moving his arms and legs)* Thank you.

LEPER *(feeling sorry)* You feel very cold, don't you?

JESUS *(smiling)* This is nothing to me. Rather, I feel cool.

LEPER But, you feel cold, surely. *(taking off his rags, he puts it on Jesus)* I've nothing but this. This may protect you, at least, from the icy wind.

JESUS I'll never forget your help.

LEPER I'll never forget your grace, my Lord, even risking my life. Because I became a really new man.

JESUS *(indicating the bronze lumps)* Take away those false skins of mine. Sell them to buy your necessary things.

LEPER Above all, I'll help my beggar friend first. From now on I'll devote my whole life for the help of the other lepers. *(kneels)* Jesus Christ, my Lord, I... I really...

JESUS I know your heart. Very good! Truly, very good! *(putting his hands on the leper's head, he blesses)* Receive my blessing and go in peace. *(gathering*

예수 (팔 다리를 움직이며) 고맙소.

문둥이 (미안해서) 춥지 않으세요?

예수 (미소를 띠며) 이 정도야… 시원하오.

문둥이 그래도 추우실 텐데… (누더기 겉옷을 벗어 예수에게 걸쳐 준다) 가진 게 이것뿐이에요. 이거라도 바람을 조금 막아 줄 거예요.

예수 당신의 도움은 영원히 잊지 않겠소.

문둥이 주님의 은총, 죽어도 잊지 않겠습니다. 전 정말 새 사람이 됐으니까요.

예수 (구리 무더기를 가리키며) 자, 저 껍데기들을 가져가시오. 팔아서 요긴한 데 쓰시오.

문둥이 친구 거지를 먼저 도와줘야겠어요. 앞으로는 문둥이를 돕는 일에 일생을 바치겠습니다. (무릎을 꿇고) 주 예수님, 전…전…

예수 잘 알았소. (두 손을 문둥이 머리에 얹어 축복하며) 나의 축복을 받으시오. 편안히 가시오. (문둥이가 구리 덩어리들을 끌어 모아 질질 끌며 왼쪽으로 나가며 예수를 한두 번 뒤돌아본다. 사이) 이제는 가짜들을 교회에서 몰아낼 시간이다.

the bronze lumps, the leper drags them and goes out to the left. He looks Jesus once again over his shoulder. Pause.) Now is the time to drive those false Christians out of my church. I'll severely punish those who praise me only with their lips, and those who turn their faces about from the practice of love. No exception.

The Priest comes out from the right humming a pop song.

PRIEST *(aside)* Oh, how wonderful the dinner was at Chairman Kim's house! The roasted chicken and spiced duck, they were the best dishes of specialty. La-la-la-ra.

SISTER *(coming out from the left)* Good night, Father.

PRIEST Good night, Sister. Everything's all right?

SISTER Yes, Father. *(seeing Jesus, She is suddenly startled)* Oh, my God!

PRIEST *(surprised at th same time)* How on earth such a thing happened! *(approaches Jesus)* These dirty rags... *(kicks the local wine bottle)* They stole away with a drink. Pshaw! What did the police do? Sleeping? Damn the police!

입으로만 나를 찬미하는 자, 사랑의 실천을 외면하는 자, 남김없이 혼을 내 줘야지.

신부가 오른쪽에서 콧노래를 부르며 나온다.

신부 (혼잣말로) 아, 김사장네 통닭구이하고 오리고기, 거 진미 중의 진미였어. 라라라라라.

수녀 (왼쪽에서 마주 오다가 신부를 보고) 이제 오세요, 신부님?

신부 아, 네, 별일 없었지요?

수녀 네. (문득 예수를 보자 놀라며) 앗!

신부 (동시에 놀라며) 아니! (예수에게 다가간다) 이 누더기는… (소주병을 발로 차며) 술 마시며 훔쳐갔군. 쳇! 도대체 경찰은 뭘 하고 있는 거야?

Sister *(in a hysterical tone)* They took away the gold crown, stick and clothes of Jesus Our Lord. What impudent thieves they are! All the saints help me! *(crosses herself.)*

Striking the leper with his baton, the policeman enters from the left. The gilded crown in his hand, the leper dodges the baton.

Policeman Still you say you didn't steal? Then, what's that you are holding in your hand? You shameless thief!

Priest *(very glad to see the policeman)* Oh, you already arrested the thief!

Sister *(crossing herself again)* Praised be Jesus!

Policeman *(to the priest)* Ah, you are here, Father. *(indicating the leper with his baton)* Well, Father, this cursed leper committed theft so fantastic. If I didn't catch him in the street, you'd suffer a tremendous loss.

Priest Well done.

Sister *(kneels before Jesus)* Praised be Jesus! Praised be Jesus!

수녀 (신경질적인 목소리로) 예수님의 금관, 지팡이, 옷을 훔쳐 가다니! 원, 세상에 이런 도둑이 다 있나? (가슴에 성호를 긋는다)

왼쪽에서 경찰이 문둥이를 방망이로 때리면서 들어온다. 구리관을 한 손에 든 문둥이가 방망이를 피한다.

경찰 도둑질을 안 했다구? 그 손에 든 건 뭐야? 이 날도둑놈아!

신부 (반색을 하며) 아, 범인을 잡아왔군요!

수녀 (성호를 그으며) 찬미 예수!

경찰 (신부에게) 신부님, 여기 계셨군요. (방망이로 문둥이를 가리키며) 아니 글쎄, 이 문둥이 자식이 엄청난 도둑질을 했지 뭡니까? 제가 마침 길에서 잡았으니 망정이지 하마터면 큰일 날 뻔했습니다.

신부 잘 하셨습니다.

수녀 (예수를 향해 무릎을 꿇으며) 찬미 예수! 찬미 예수!

Leper *(tries to protest, but in a weak tone)* I'm not a leper anymore. I didn't steal either.

Policeman *(wielding the baton)* How dare you son of a bitch start a lie again?

Leper I say the truth, not a lie.

Priest *(to the leper)* Repent of your sin! Shame on you to steal these sacred articles!

Policeman *(hitting the leper)* Bring back every item you took away, you cursed stinking thief! *(The leper falls down under the feet of Jesus)* Hey, you rotten rascal! This is a terribly stubborn neck. Do you think your pretending will save your neck? Nonsense! *(in a very friendly tone to the priest)* Oh, I had such a hard time bringing this rascal here, Father.

Priest *(taking out some money from his pocket, he puts it steaithily in the policeman's hand)* Many thanks for your trouble. This is very small, but...

Policeman *(pretends not to receive, but actually grabs the money)* I don't expect you, too, to give me... Father.

Priest Just a humble present of my heart.

문둥이 (힘없는 목소리로 항의하듯이) 전 문둥이가 아닙니다. 도둑질도 안 했어요.

경찰 (방망이를 휘두르며) 이 자식이 어따 대고 또 거짓말이야?

문둥이 정말입니다.

신부 (문둥이에게) 참회하시오. 신성한 물건을 훔치다니!

경찰 (문둥이를 때리며) 훔친 물건을 모조리 제자리에 갖다 놔! 이 도둑놈아! (문둥이가 예수의 발 아래 쓰러진다) 어어, 이거 봐라. 아주 지독한 자식이군. 너 엄살 떨면 단 줄 알아? (신부에게 은근한 목소리로) 아, 이놈 잡아 오느라고 혼이 났습니다, 신부님.

신부 (주머니에서 슬며시 돈을 꺼내 경찰 손에 쥐어 주며) 정말 수고 많았습니다. 이거 약소하지만….

경찰 (못 이기는 척하고 받으며) 신부님까지 이러실 건 없는데…

신부 그저 성의니까요.

Leper *(still prostrating)* I never stole this. Jesus himself gave it to me.

Priest *(stupefied)* What? Jesus himself gave it to you? *(bursts out laughing)* Ha, ha, ha, ha! That statue gave it to you? You are crazy, hopelessly insane!

Policeman *(to the priest)* Yes, this foul stinking leper is completely mad. Impossible to cure. *(kicks, violently, the leper's side with the tip of his shoes)* How dare you make fools of us? You cursed rat! I'll teach you a lesson tonight.

Leper *(shrieking, he lies flat on his back)* Ouch! Ouch! He kills me. I'm dying.

Policeman *(kicks again)* Don't make a great fuss here. *(the leper doesn't react)*

Priest *(to the policeman)* Now, it's enough. I'm satisfied to get back the stolen things.

Policeman This is a very unusual thief. Stripping the bronze statue of Jesus, of all the others...

Priest People's hearts grow worse and worse. I shouldn't be surprised, if more horrible things happen from now. Ah, what kind of world are we living in!

문둥이 (엎드린 채) 이건 훔친 게 아닙니다. 예수님께서 직접 주신 거예요.

신부 (기가 막혀서) 뭐? 예수님께서 직접 줘? (폭소하며) 하하하하. 저 동상이 그걸 주었다고? 돌아도 단단히 돌았군.

경찰 (신부에게) 미쳐도 여간 미친 게 아닌 모양입니다. (구둣발로 문둥이를 세게 걷어차며) 이 자식이 누굴 놀려? 이게! 너 아직 정신 못 차렸냐?

문둥이 (비명을 지르며 고꾸라진다) 아이쿠! 나 죽는다.

경찰 (한 번 더 걷어차며) 엄살 떨지 마! (문둥이가 잠잠하다)

신부 (경찰에게) 자, 자, 그만해 두십시오. 잃어버린 물건을 되찾게 되었으니 안심입니다.

경찰 별 걸 다 훔쳐 가려고 했습니다요. 하…하필이면 예수 동상을 벗겨서…

신부 세상 인심이 갈수록 난폭해지니 앞으로 무슨 일이 터질는지, 원.

Jesus *(stepping down the pedestal)* I did give it to him. *(Startled, the sister rose up. The priest and policeman are surprised, too, and they stood back a few steps. Pause. Taking off the rags, Jesus covers the leper with it. Jesus looks at them with glaring eyes. then, pointing at them with his finger)* You are a priest. You are a sister. You are a policeman. All of you, how can you do these things? Even if I appeal the truth to your conscience that's already polluted by hypocrisy and injustice, what's the use of it? You make so much noise that you are my disciples, but you never try to practise my teachings, not even a single one. All of you false Christians are fake, and truly my shame! A heavy yoke on my neck! *(indicating the leper)* Look at this man! Look, he fell down exhausted by your contemptuous treatment, indifference and abuse! While he begged you to relieve him from sharp hunger, you turned about your face. Oh, you vipers!

Priest *(tries to protest)* Jesus my Lord! You don't need to interfere in our worldly affairs.

Policeman *(indicating the leper)* This is a thief.

예수 (받침대에서 내려서며) 내가 주었소! (수녀가 깜짝 놀라 일어선다. 신부와 경찰도 놀라 한 걸음 물러선다. 사이. 예수가 누더기를 벗어 쓰러진 문둥이를 덮어준다. 예수가 찬찬히 세 사람을 노려보다가 일일이 손가락질하며) 신부, 수녀, 경찰, 당신네 양심에 내가 진리를 호소한들 무슨 소용이 있겠소? 입으로는 나의 제자라고 떠들면서도 나의 가르침은 하나도 실천하려 들지 않는 당신네 껍데기 신자들은 나의 수치요. 내 목에 걸린 멍에란 말이요. (문둥이를 가리키며) 보시오, 이 사람을! 이 사람이 배고파 구걸할 때 당신들은 외면했소. 에이, 독사의 무리 같으니!

신부 (항의하듯) 예수님! 이런 속세의 일은 당신이 참견할 게 못 됩니다.

경찰 (문둥이를 가리키며) 이놈은 도둑입니다.

Jesus I said I gave these to him.

Priest Who told you to give him? These bronze articles were prepared by the collection of my parishioners. Jesus my Lord, you'd better just stand still and look.

Jesus You order me just to look? I can't do that. Never! It's against my teaching. Now I can't entrust my sheep any more to you hypocrites. *(slowly goes to the left)*

Priest Quo vadis, Domine? *(Where are you going, my Lord?)*

Jesus I'm going to my sheep. I'm now going to those who recognise my voice and practise my teaching. I am a good shepherd. From now on I myself will lead them. I don't need such people who cover me with useless sheets of bronze and pray before a dead statue anymore. The poor and the abandoned people are crushed by pain and groaning. This pitiful people, my people, cry out to me. I can't pretend not to hear their groans and cries any more. Don't you remember I am the good shepherd? *(pause)* I will teach them myself.

예수 내가 주었다니까!

신부 누가 주라고 했습니까? 이 물건은 신자들 헌금으로 만든 것이고… 예수님께선 그저 가만히 계십시오.

예수 나더러 가만히 구경이나 하라고? 천만에! 그건 안 될 노릇이지. 당신네 같은 위선자들에게 더 이상 내 양떼를 내맡길 수가 없소. (천천히 왼쪽으로 걸음을 옮긴다)

신부 주님, 어디로 가시렵니까?

예수 내 양떼를 치러 가오. 내 음성을 알아듣고 내 말을 실천하는 사람들을 인도하러 가겠소. 나는 착한 목자요. 나에게 이따위 구리껍데기나 씌우고 그 앞에서 기도하는 사람은 필요가 없소. 가난하고 버림받은 사람들이 고통에 못 이겨 내지르는 저 신음소리, 저 가련한 백성의 부르짖음을 더 이상 내가 못 들은 척할 수가 없소. 나는 착한 목자란 말이오. (사이) 내가 직접 가르치겠소.

When Jesus goes out to the left, the sister prays urgently with her hands clasped, the policeman yawns absent-mindedly and the priest, making a peculiar gesture, continuously talks to himself incomprehensibly. The leper rises up slowly and, raising the crown high, follows the footsteps of Jesus. A bell rings. The sister and policeman go out to the right. Pause.

Priest *(aside)* Did I have a dream? Or was I enchanted by a devil? *(slowly wandering on the stage)* It is the night of confusion and pain. Now is the time of the most terrible darkness. But the night passes, and the dawn surely comes. When the dawn arrives, people will be ashamed of their own figure which they see in the mirror. Ashamed? Will they be really? *(a bell rings more loudly)* Oh, that sound of the bell...

All characters come out to the stage from the left and the right singing in a chorus the title song "Jesus of the Gold Crown".

The curtain does not fall.

⟨*BEGINNING*⟩

예수가 왼쪽으로 걸어 나갈 때 수녀는 합장한 채 열심히 기도하고, 경찰은 멍청한 표정으로 하품을 한다. 신부는 괴상한 몸짓에다가 알아들을 수 없는 소리를 혼자 마구 지껄여대고, 느린 동작으로 일어선 문둥이가 금관을 높이 쳐들고 예수의 뒤를 따른다. 종소리가 울려 퍼진다. 수녀와 경찰이 오른쪽으로 나간다. 사이.

신부 (혼잣말로) 내가 꿈을 꾸었나? 아니면, 도깨비에게 홀렸나? (느린 걸음으로 무대를 거닐며) 혼란과 고통의 밤이다. 지금은 캄캄한 암흑의 시간, 그러나 밤이 지나면 반드시 새벽이 온다. 새벽이 오면 사람들이 거울에 비친 자기 모습을 보고 부끄러워하겠지. 아니, 정말 부끄러워할까? (종소리가 들린다) 아, 저 종소리…

나오는 사람들이 무대 좌우에서 천천히 걸어 나오면서 김민기 작사 작곡인 '금관의 예수'를 합창한다.

막은 내리지 않는다.

시작.

작품을 쓰고 나서

이 희곡은 1971년 12월 31일 하룻밤에 전부 쓴 것이다. 탈고한 직후 나는 다음과 같이 솔직한 심정을 적었다.

현재 한국가톨릭이 당면하고 있는 문제 가운데 가장 심각한 문제는 그리스도의 사랑과 정의 안에서 생생하게 신앙을 생활화하지 못하고 있는 것이다. 그 원인이 어디 있는가를 반성하는 데조차 게으름을 보이고 있는 현실이 안타깝기만 하다. 이러한 생각에서 나는 그리스도의 참 모습을 추구하여 보았다.

어느 정도 그 생각이 구체적으로 표현되었는지는 몰라도 가능한 한 진실하게 그것을 나타내려고 했음은 사실이다.

입으로만 주를 섬기는 사람이 사라지고, 정말로 그

리스도의 가르침이 하나의 장식품이 되지 말고 살아 있는 신앙의 기초가 되기를 기원한다. 행동이 없는 신앙은 죽은 신앙이라고 한 사도의 말을 명심하면서….

1971.12.31. 서울 창천동에서

*

추기:

18년이 지난 오늘 이 희곡을 다시 정리하면서 나는 우리 사회가 또 한국교회가 물질적인 면에서 어느 정도 풍요로움을 누리게 되기는 했으나 아직 어두운 구석을 적지 않게 간직하고 있는 현실을 발견하면서 씁쓸한 감회를 억누를 길이 없다. 물질적 빈곤이나 육체적 억압보다도 정신적 빈곤과 영혼의 황폐가 더 참혹하다는 것을 지난 18년간의 세월이 우리에게 가르쳐

주려 했는데도, 우리가 과거를 통해 얼마만큼 교훈을 받았는지는 미지수이다.

하여간 이 희곡의 공연이 환영을 받고 또 관객에게 감동을 주면 줄수록 그 사회는 병이 깊이 든 사회라는 사실을 반추하면서, 작가로서 보람과 아울러 비애를 느낀다. 나는 차라리 이 희곡이 무시되는 사회가 하루 빨리 우리 땅에 실현되기를 바란다.

1989.2.21. 네덜란드 헤이그에서

이동진 작가 연보

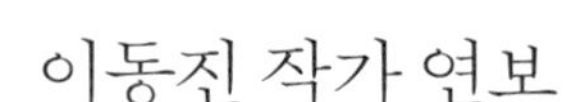

1945년 황해도 신천군 남부면 비봉리 출생

1948년 서울 거주(영등포구 상도동)

1950년 대구 거주(대명동 피난민촌)

1952년 대구 복명초등학교 입학

1955년 서울 강남초등학교 전학(상도동)

1961년 경기중학교 졸업(2월)
시 〈나는 바다로 가지 않을 테야〉 발표(2월, 교지 "경기" 제2호)

1964년 성신고등학교 (小신학교) 졸업

1964년 가톨릭대학 (신학교) 철학과 입학

1965년 성균관대학교 영문과 2학년 편입

1966년 서울대 법과대학 법학과 입학
시 〈'앙젤루우즈'를 울리라는〉 발표, 서울대 교지 大學新聞 (8.29.)
시 〈갈색 어항 속의 의식〉 발표, 대학신문(11.7)

1967년 단편소설 〈위선자, 그 이야기〉 발표(10월, 법대 교지 Fides)
시 〈10월의 대지–광시곡 1〉 발표, 대학신문(10.2.)

1968년 단편소설 〈최후 법정〉 발표(2월, Fides)
학훈단 (R.O.T.C.) 간부 후보생(3월)
『가톨릭시보』 현상문예작품모집 시 당선(10월)

1969년 시 〈韓의 숲〉 발표(현대문학 5월호)
제2회 외무고시 합격(6월)
학훈단 (R.O.T.C.) 간부 후보생, 폐결핵으로 제적(8월)
외무부 근무 개시 (9월, 외무사무관)
시 〈눈물〉 발표, 대학신문(6.2.)
시 〈지혜의 뜰〉 발표, 대학신문(9.1.)
시 〈비극의 낙엽을 쓸어내는 시간〉, 대학신문(12.15.)
제1 시집 《韓의 숲》 발간(12월, 지학사)

1970년 〈현대문학〉 시 추천 3회 완료로 등단(2월, 추천위원 박두진)

서울대 법과대학 법학과 졸업(2월)
서울대 경영대학원 입학(3월)
월간 상아(象牙) 창간, 편집장(6월, 발행인: 나상조 신부)

1971년 월간 상아 폐간(2월, 발행인이 교회 내부 사정으로 사퇴)
극단 〈상설무대〉 창단, 극단 대표(3월)
제2 시집 《쌀의 문화》 발간(5월, 삼애사)
희곡 〈베라크루스〉 공연 (6월, 극단 상설무대, 혜화동 소재 가톨릭학생회관)
희곡 〈써머스쿨〉 공연(11월, 극단 상설무대, 가톨릭학생회관)

1972년 주일대사관 근무(2등서기관, 영사)
희곡 〈금관의 예수〉 공연(2월~3월, 극단 상설무대)
– 서강대학교 캠퍼스 야외 초연(2월), 서울 드라마센터 공연 이후 1개월간 전국 순회공연 실시
– 관련 기사 : 가톨릭시보(3.12.), "풍자극 금관의 예수, 위선적 그리스도인을 질책", 유치진 연극평 "간결해도 깊은 우수작, 격하돼가는 교회 신랄히 비판"
극단 〈상설무대〉 해산(12월)

1976년 외무부 아주국 동북아1과 근무(2월, 외무서기관)
장편소설 《그림자만 풍경화》 출간(11월, 세종출판공사)

1977년 희곡집 《독신자 아파트》 출간(3월, 세종출판공사)
희곡 〈카인의 빵〉 공연(6월, 충남대 한밭극회)
희곡 〈독신자 아파트〉 공연(12월, 강원대 극단 영그리 26)

1978년 외무부 법무담당관(3월), 행정관리담당관(9월)
제3 시집 《우리 겨울 길》 출간(3월, 신서각)
번역 《나를 찾아서》 출간(9월, 웨인 W. 다이어, 자유문학사)
번역 《버찌로 가득 찬 세상》 출간(12월, 에마 봄베크, 자유문학사)
기증: 극단 "연우무대"에 연극관련 외국어 서적 200여권 기증(12월)

1979년 번역 《미래의 확신》 출간(1월, 허먼 칸, 자유문학사)
제4 시집 《뒤집어 입을 수도 없는 영혼》 출간(1월, 자유문학사)
희곡 〈자고 니러 우는 새야〉 발표 (1월, 심상사, 별책 부록)
인터뷰: 경향신문(1.10.), "시집, 희곡집, 번역서 등 출간"
희곡 〈배비장 알비장〉 공연 (3월~4월, 극단 민예, 이대 앞 민예극장)
인터뷰: 일간 스포츠(4.21.), 선데이 서울(5.6.)
희곡집 《당신은 천사가 아냐》 출간(3월, 심상사)
희곡집 《참 특이한 환자》 출간(3월, 심상사)
주이탈리아 대사관 근무(4월, 참사관)
번역 《왜 사는가 왜 죽는가》 출간(9월, 죤 포우웰, 자유문학사)

1980년 제5 시집 《꿈과 희망 사이》 출간(5월, 심상사)
번역 《하느님, 오, 하느님》 출간(8월, 죤 포우웰, 지유문학사)

1981년 이탈리아어로 번역된 시 5편 특집 게재(문학 및 정치평론 월간지 L'Osservatore Politico Letterario, 1월호)
– 관련 기사: 한국일보 및 일간스포츠(2.27.);
서울신문 및 경향신문(3.3.); 조선일보(3.5.); 문학사상 4월호
제6 시집 《Sunshines on Peninsula》 출간(3월, Pioneer Publishing Co., LA)
번역 《왜 사랑하기를 두려워하는가》 출간(4월, 죤 포우웰, 자유문학사)
국제극예술협회(I.T.I.) 마드리드 총회, 한국대표단 참가(6월)
이탈리아 시인 쥬세페 롱고(Giuseppe Longo)의 시 5편 번역 발표
(심상, 7월호)
기행문집 《천사가 그대를 낙원으로》 출간(이탈리아 및 유럽 기행문집, 9월, 우신사)
주바레인 대사관 근무 (9월, 참사관)
개인 영어 시화전 개최 (10월, 장소: 로마 Galleria Astrolabio Arte)

1982년 인터뷰 : 바레인 영어일간지 Gulf Daily News(6.2.), 영역 시 3편 게재
번역 《악마의 사전》 출간(9월, 앰브로즈 비어스, 우신사)
번역 《교황님의 구두》 출간(11월, 모리스 웨스트, 우신사)
바레인 시인 이브라힘 알 아라예드(Ibrahim Al Arrayed) 대사의 詩論
"컴뮤니케이숀의 단계, 시인과 수학자" 번역 발표(심상, 11월호)

1983년 사우디 아라비아 시인 가지 알고사이비(Ghazi A.Algosaibi) 대사의
시집 "동방과 사막으로부터" 번역 발표(심상, 4월호.)
번역 《악마의 변호인》 출간(6월, 모리스 웨스트, 우신사)
제7 시집 《신들린 세월》 출간(7월, 우신사)

1984년 단편소설 〈자유의 대가(代價)〉 발표(주부생활, 3월호)
희곡 〈배비장 알비장〉 공연(12월, 극단 노라)

1985년 제8 시집 《Agony with Pride》 출간(1월, Al Hilal Middle East Co.Ltd., Cyprus)
– 관련 기사: 코리아 헤랄드(2.20.), 코리아 타임즈(2.26.)
인터뷰: 경향신문(3.15.), 조선일보(3.19.)
단편소설 〈허망한 매듭〉 발표(소설문학, 2월호)
단편소설집 《로마에서 띄운 작은 풍선》 출간(5월, 자유문학사)
– 관련 서평: 주간 조선(10.13.)
사진집 〈Rhapsody in Nature〉에 영역 시 10편 발표(9월, 서울국제출판사)
인터뷰: 소설문학(10월호), "외교관 작가"
번역 《예수님의 광고술》 출간(11월, 브루스 바톤, 우신사)

1986년 번역 《매디슨카운티의 추억》 출간(2월, 제이나 세인트 제임스, 문학수첩)
번역 《장미의 이름으로》 출간(3월, 움베르토 에코, 우신사, 국내 최초 번역)
하버드대 국제문제연구소 연구원(Fellow), 외무부 파견 연수(6월)
제9 시집 《이동진 대표시 선집》 출간(8월, 동산출판사)
제10 시집 《마음은 강물》 출간(8월, 동산출판사)
제8 시집 《Agony with Pride》 국내 출간(8월, 서울국제출판사)
번역 《이탈리아 민화집》 출간(10월, 이탈로 칼비노, 샘터사)
번역 《덴마크 민화집》 출간(12월, 스벤트 그룬트비히, 샘터사)
번역 《하느님의 어릿광대》 출간(12월, 모리스 웨스트, 삼신각)

1987년 뉴질랜드 시인 루이스 존슨(Louis Johnson) 의 시 5편 및 미국 여시인 패트리셔 핑켈(Patrisia Garfingkel)의 시 7편 번역 발표(심상, 2월호)
주네덜란드 대사관 근무(6월, 참사관)
희곡 번역: 빌 C.데이비스 작, 매스 어필(Mass Appeal), 극단 바탕골 창단기념 공연(9월)

1988년 번역 《아버지에게, 아들에게》 출간(5월, 엘모 줌발트 2세, 삼신각)
인터뷰: 네덜란드 격월간지 Driemaster(5월호)
제11 시집 《객지의 꿈》 출간(8월, 청하사)
제12 시집 《담배의 기도》 출간(11월, 혜진서관)

1989년 영역 시 11편 발표(Korea Journal, 5월호, 7월호)
장편소설 《우리가 사랑하는 죄인》 출간(5월, 삼신각)
– KBS TV, 12부작 미니시리즈로 제작, 1990.8~10.방영, 1991.2. 재방영
인터뷰 특집: 주간조선(8.6.), "인간 내면과 공직 수행"
중편소설 〈암스텔담 공항〉 발표 (민족지성, 10월호)
중편소설 〈펭귄과 갈매기의 대화〉 발표 (민족지성, 12월호)
희곡 〈금관의 예수〉, 한국 희곡작가 협회, "1989년도 연간 희곡집"에 수록

1990년 제13 시집 《바람 부는 날의 은총》 출간(1월, 문학아카데미)
주일 대사관 근무 (3월, 총영사)
번역 《무자격 부모》 출간(5월, 삼신각)
번역 《중국 황금살인 사건》 출간(7월, 로베르트 반 훌릭, 삼신각)
대담 특집 : 일본 마이니찌 신문 논설부위원장과 대담(언론과 비평, 8월호)
인터뷰 특집: 일본의 인기가수 아그네스 챤이 취재 (일본 월간지 "家庭の友", 10월호)
인터뷰: 시사 저널(10.4.), "우리가 사랑하는 죄인 소설의 원작자"
– 관련 기사: 일간스포츠(8.2.); 조선일보(8.22.); 국민일보(9.2.)
장편소설 《민주화 십자군》 출간(11월, 삼신각)
제14 시집 《아름다운 평화》 출간(12월, 언론과 비평사)
희곡 〈베라크루스〉, 한국 희곡작가 협회, "1990년도 연간 희곡집"에 수록

1991년 희곡 〈베라크루스〉 발표(월간 민족지성 1월호)
인터뷰: 일본 일간지 東洋經濟日報 (7.26.)
희곡집 《누더기 예수》 출간(8월, 동산출판사)
– 관련 기사: 동아일보(8.8.),"희곡 금관의 예수 원작자"; 가톨릭신문(9.1.)
인터뷰: 국민일보(8.17.), "문화 외교, 희곡 금관의 예수";
일간스포츠(8.19.) ; 코리아 타임즈(8.22.)
번역 《꼬마 호비트의 모험》 출간(8월, J.R.R.톨키엔, 성바오로출판사)
주벨기에 대사관 근무(9월, 공사)
번역 《귀향》 출간(11월, 앤 타일러, 삼신각)
번역 《이런 사람이 무자격 부모다》 출간(12월, 수잔 포워드, 삼신각)

1992년 세계시인대회 (벨기에 리에쥬), 한국대표로 참가(9월)
– 주제 발표:한국 시의 현황
번역 《성난 지구》 출간(10월, 아이작 아시모프, 삼신각)
번역 《마술반지(1)》 출간(11월, J.R.R. 톨키엔, 성바오로출판사)

1993년 번역 《꼬마 호비트의 모험》 출간(2월, 톨키엔, 성바오로출판사)
인터뷰: 국민일보(2.2.), "문화 알려야"
국방대학원 안보과정, 외무부 파견 연수(2월)
– 논문 "미국 신행정부의 대한 외교정책 연구" 발표
인터뷰: 주간조선(3.4.), "외교관 시인"
제15 시집 《우리가 찾아내야 할 사람》 출간(3월, 성 바오로 출판사)
인터뷰 특집: 월간 퀸(4월호), "금관의 예수 원작자"
인터뷰: 스포츠서울(8.4.), "현직외교관 47권 출간"
인터뷰: 주간여성(8.26.), "이런 남자"
외무부 외교안부연구원 근무(12월, 연구관)

1994년 번역 《숨겨진 성서 1, 2, 3(전 3권)》 출간(1월, 3월, 윌리스 반스토운, 문학수첩)
번역 《마술반지(2)》 출간(1월, 톨키엔, 성바오로출판사)
수필 〈동숭동 캠퍼스의 추억과 나의 길〉 발표(1월, 서울대 법대 동창 수상록(2) 하늘이 무너져도 정의는 세워라, 경세원)
번역 《희망의 북쪽》 출간(2월, 존 헤슬러, 우리시대사)
번역 《일본을 벗긴다》 출간(5월, 가와사키 이치로, 문학수첩)
번역 《Starlights of Nirvana》(석용산 시선집 "열반의 별빛") 영역 출간 (12월, 문학수첩)

1995년 번역 《지상 60센티미터 위를 걸으며》 출간(3월, 미국 시인협회 회장 제노 플래티 시집, 책만드는 집)
대구시 국제관계 자문대사(4월)
중편소설 〈추억의 유전〉 발표(계간 작가세계, 95. 여름호)

번역 《공포 X 파일》 출간(7월, 추리단편선, 문학수첩)
번역 《괴기 X 파일》 출간(7월, 추리단편선, 문학수첩)
제16 시집 《오늘 내게 잠시 머무는 행복》 출간(10월, 문학수첩)
칼람 연재 : 동아일보, "이 생각 저 생각" 주간연재(1월~4월)
매일신문, "매일춘추" 주간연재(5월~6월)
주간 불교, "세간과 출세간 사이" 주간연재(6월)
라디오 대담: MBC-FM, "여성시대"(11.25. 사회: 손숙)

1996년 번역 《에로 판타지아 1, 2 (전2권)》 출간(1월, 단편소설집, 문학수첩)
번역 《매디슨 카운티의 다리, 그 추억》 출간(2월, 제이나 세인트 제임스, 문학수첩)
라디오 대담: KBS 제2라디오(2.1.), "한밤에 만난 사람 대담"(사회: 박범신)
교통방송(2.27.), "임국희 대담, 라디오광장"
번역 《학교에서 일어나는 폭력문제》 출간(3월, 단 올베우스, 삼신각)
주나이지리아 대사 부임(3월), 주시에라 레온, 주카메룬, 주챠드 대사(겸임)
시집 〈Agony With Pride〉 서평, 나이지리아 일간지 The Guardian(10.14.)
시 "1달러의 행복" 영역 발표, 나이지리아 일간지 The Guardian(12.19.)

1998년 시 "1달러의 행복" 발표(월간조선, 2월호)
제17 시집 《1달러의 행복》 출간(4월, 문학수첩)
제18 시집 《지구는 한방울 눈물》 출간(4월, 동산출판사)
– 관련 기사: 중앙일보(4.28.), "현직 외교관이 펴낸 두 권의 시집"
가톨릭신문(5.17.), "일상 소재 121편 소박한 시 담아"
중앙일보(7.9.), "한국문학 세계로 날개짓"
한국일보(7.15.), "한국문학 유럽에 번역 소개"
해누리기획 출판사 공동 설립에 참여(9월)
번역 《예수 그리스도 제2복음》 출간(12월, 조제 사라마고, 문학수첩)

1999년 외교통상부 본부 대사(1월)
번역 《바로 보는 왕따: 대안은 있다》 출간(2월, 단 올베우스, 삼신각)
희곡 《Jesus of Gold Crown》(금관의 예수) 영역 출간(3월, Spectrum Books Ltd., Nigeria)
기행문집 《아웃 오브 아프리카》 출간(8월, 모아드림)
– 관련 인터뷰: KBS제1라디오 (8.28.); KBS 라디오, 봉두완 (8.30.); SBS라디오(8.31.); SBS라디오 이수경의 파워(9.5.)
제19 시집 《Songs of My Soul》 출간(10월, Peperkorn Edition, Germany)
번역 《The Floating Island》(김종철 시선집 "떠도는 섬") 영역 출간(12월, Peperkorn Edition, Germany)
희곡 〈딸아, 이제는 네 길을 가라〉 발표(화백문학 제9집, 99년 하반기호)
라디오 대담: 이케하라 마모루(맞아죽을 각오로 쓴 한국, 한국인 저자)와

한일관계 대담 1시간, 기독교방송(8.13.)
칼람 연재: 가톨릭신문, "방주의 창"(9월~12월)
인터뷰: 중앙일보(11.4.), "이득수 교수 공동 인터뷰",
조선일보(11.8.), "한국시 라틴문학론으로 포장해 유럽수출",
동아일보(11.9.), "한국문학 유럽에 소개; 교수-대사 의기투합"

2000년 평저 《에센스 삼국지》 출간(2월, 해누리출판사)
번역 《The Sea of Dandelions》(이해인 시선집 "민들레의 바다") 영역 출간(2월, Perperkorn Edition, Germany)
번역 《아담과 이브의 생애》 출간(5월, 고대문서, 해누리출판사)
대담: 평화방송 TV (6.26.), 방영 1시간, 김미진 대담, 5회 방영
인터뷰: KBS라디오(6.29), 방송 40분, 2회 방송, "나의 삶, 나의 보람", 최영미 아나운서 대담
외교통상부 퇴직 (7월)
– 관련 기사: 매일신문, 연합통신, 대한매일, 한국일보(6.26.), 뉴스피플(6.28.), "자동퇴직에 항의"
번역 《예수의 인간경영과 마케팅 전략》 출간(10월, 브루스 바톤, 해누리출판사)
번역 《예언자》 출간(10월, 칼릴 지브란, 해누리출판사)

2001년 해누리출판사 인수, 발행인(1월)
번역 《걸리버 여행기》 출간(1월, 조나탄 스위프트, 해누리출판사)
희곡 〈가장 장엄한 미사〉 발표(화백문학 제11집, 2001년 상반기 호)
번역 《제2의 성서, 신약시대, 구약시대(전 2권)》 출간(9월, 해누리출판사)
장편소설 《외교관 1, 2 (전 2권)》 출간(9월, 우리문학사)
– 관련 기사: 조선일보, 중앙일보, 세계일보(8.31.), "소설 외교관 출간, 외교부 인사정책 비판"; 동아일보(9.1.), "말, 말, 말"(소설 외교관 인용)
인터뷰: MBC 라디오 "MBC초대석 차인태입니다"(9.29.)

2002년 번역 《권력과 영광》 출간(4월, 그레이엄 그린, 해누리출판사)
번역 《이솝 우화》 출간(7월, 해누리출판사)
번역 《사포》 출간(10월, 알퐁스 도데, 해누리출판사)
번역 《군주론; 로마사 평론》 출간(12월, 마키아벨리, 해누리출판사)
수필 〈나는 부자아빠가 싫다〉 등 8편 발표(12월, 국방부 "마음의 양식" 제80집)

2003년 번역 《짜릿한 넘 하나 물어와》 출간(4월, 동화집, 해누리출판사)
특강: "21세기 문화의 흐름", 추계예술대학(4.9.)
월간 〈착한 이웃〉 창간, 발행인(5월)
– 노숙자 등을 무료로 치료하는 〈요셉의원〉 돕기 활동, 2008년 4월까지 잡지 발행, 매년 연말에 자선미술전 개최, 수익금 전액 기증

번역 《新 군주론》 출간(7월, 귀차르디니, 해누리출판사)
제20 시집 《개나라의 개나으리들》 출간(9월, 해누리출판사)

2004년 번역 《Sunlight on the Land Far From Home》(홍윤숙 시선집 "타관의햇살") 영역 출간(1월, Perperkorn Edition, Germany)
편저 《동서양의 고사성어》 출간(3월, 해누리출판사)
편저 《동서양의 천자문》 출간(4월, 해누리출판사)
번역 《세상의 지혜》 출간(4월, 발타사르 그레시안, 해누리출판사)
장편소설 《사랑은 없다》 출간(12월, 해누리출판사)

2005년 번역 《주님과 똑같이》 출간(3월, 성 샤를 드 푸코 일기, 해누리출판사)
편저 《세계명화성서, 신약, 구약(전 2권)》 출간(5월, 해누리출판사)
제15회 한국가톨릭 매스컴상, 출판부문상 수상 (12월)

2006년 번역 《아무도 모르는 예수》 출간(3월, 해누리출판사)

2007년 편역 《세계의 명언 1,2(전 2권)》 출간(1월, 해누리출판사)
서평: 《세계의 명언》, 배인준 칼럼, 동아일보(2.27.)
인터뷰 특집: "우리들의 '착한 이웃' 이동진 시인", 글 박경희, 방송문예(4월호)
특강: "이웃에게 봉사하는 삶", 레이크사이드 CC(5.7.)
제21 시집 《사람의 아들은 이렇게 말했다》 출간(6월, 해누리출판사)
번역 《링컨의 일생》 출간(8월, 에밀 루드비히, 해누리출판사)
번역 《천로역정》 출간(12월, 존 번연, 해누리출판사)

2008년 번역 《좋은 왕 나쁜 왕-帝鑑圖說》 출간(1월, 중국고전, 해누리출판사)
편저 《에센스 명화 성경-구약 1,2, 신약 1,2 (전 4권)》 출간(1월, 해누리출판사)
서평: "에센스 명화성경-구약 1,2, 신약 1,2 (전 4권) 발간", 가톨릭시보(2.17)
월간 〈착한 이웃〉 폐간(4월)
번역 《터키인들의 유머》 출간(8월, 해누리출판사)

2009년 제22 시집 《Songs of My Soul》 출간(11월, 해누리출판사)
제23 시집 《내 영혼의 노래-등단 40주년 기념시집》 출간(11월, 해누리출판사)
번역 《명상록》 출간(9월, 아우렐리우스, 해누리출판사)

2010년 번역 《성서 우화》 출간(1월, 중세 유럽 우화집 "Gesta Romanorum"의 국내 최초 번역, 해누리출판사)
《A Review of Korean History 1, 2, 3 (전 3권)》(한영우 저, "다시 찾는 한국역사") 영어 감수 및 일부분 영역, 출간(1월, 경세원)
번역 《365일 에센스 톨스토이 잠언집》 출간(7월, 톨스토이, 해누리출판사)

2011년 칼럼 연재: 원자력위원회 회보 "원우"(1월~12월)
일본 일간지에 이동진 소개 칼럼: "브랏셀의 가을", 글 오이카와 고조, 日本經濟新聞(3.2.)

2012년 인터뷰 특집: “책벌레 외교관 30년, 책장수는 내 운명”, 일간 아시아경제(9.11)
인터뷰 특집: “출판사대표가 된 전직 대사 이동진”, 기아자동차 사보 “마침표”(12월호)

2014년 번역 《Rose Stone in Arabian Sand》(신기섭 시집 “사막의 장미) 영역 출간(3월, 해누리출판사)
편저 《영어속담과 천자문》 출간(8월, 해누리출판사)
제24 시집 《개나라에도 봄은 오는가》 출간(12월, 해누리출판사)

2015년 대화마당 “공영방송, 국민의 기대와 KBS의 현실”에 질문자로 참여(5.16~28., 주최 KBS이사회)
편저 《영어속담과 고사성어》 출간(7월, 해누리출판사)
번역 《성공 커넥션》 출간(12월, 제시 워렌 티블로우, 이너북)

2017년 제25 시집 《굿 모닝, 커피!》 출간(12월, 해누리출판사)
번역 《영어속담과 함께 읽는 세상의 지혜》 출간(2월, 발타사르 그라시안, 해누리출판사)

2018년 번역 《역사를 바꾼 세계 영웅사》 출간(7월, 해누리출판사)

2019년 번역 《세상을 어떻게 이해할 것인가》 출간(1월, 니체, 해누리출판사)
번역 《1분 군주론》 출간(8월, 마키아벨리, 해누리출판사)
제26 시집 《얼빠진 세상–등단 50주년 기념시집》 출간(12월, 해누리출판사)

2020년 제27 시집 《얼빠진 시대–등단 50주년 기념시집》 출간(4월, 해누리출판사)

2021년 평역 《한 권으로 읽는 밀레니얼 삼국지》 출간(7월, 해누리출판사)
인터뷰: “칠십 평생 직업만 다섯 개, 이동진 전 대사가 사는 법”, 조선일보(4.24.)
제28 시집 《얼빠진 나라–등단 50주년 기념시집》 출간(11월, 해누리출판사)